Other Books by Dan Norvell and Larry Eissler:

Ghosts of the Black Hawk War

Paranormal Theories: A Logical Approach

ANTHOLOGY

DAN NORVELL

WITH LARRY EISSLER

First Edition:
First printing

PUBLISHED BY HAUNTED ROAD MEDIA, LLC
www.hauntedroadmedia.com

United States of America

Acknowledgments

We would like to thank the following individuals who helped bring this book to life:

The Norvell Family. Dan's family has been a primary supporter of his desire to write the stories featured in this book. Without their loving support, Dan's dream of publishing this book may not have been possible.

Sandra and Russ Wells. Sandra and Russ have been long time friends of Dan and Larry. In 2011, Dan and Sandra co-authored a book of short stories together titled, *Beyond Life: The Ghost Chronicles*. It was this book, and Dan's short stories within it, that introduced Dan's unique writing style of telling ghost stories from the ghost's perspective to his readers. Without the support of the Wells, Dan's story telling talent may never have been realized.

Amelia Cotter. Thanks to Amelia, we have found ourselves on this wonderful road to being published authors and members of the incredible Haunted Road Media family.

Mike Ricksecker and Haunted Road Media. Thank you for accepting this anthology of ghost stories so quickly after publishing our other book, Ghosts of the Black Hawk War. The Haunted Road Media family is full of credible, talented authors and to be counted among them is an honor we will never forget.

Table of Contents

Introduction

These stories you are about to read are fictional stories that I have brought to you from thoughts that I have had during my experiences from investigating the paranormal and in life. There are many of these stories that have a good vs. evil undertone in them. What I have tried to do with these stories is to show you the reader that everything is a choice. The choices we make can have a positive or negative effect on not only the lost souls in these stories, but to those that are left behind as well. There are many stories out there that feature ghosts and spirits, but many of them do not look at the world that remains through the ghosts' eyes. With these stories, that is what I have done. I wanted you all to take a unique journey with these departed souls and follow them through the navigation of the afterlife. Some ghosts in more stories find out that even though they are dead, they still have much to contribute to the people that they left behind. Some of these ghosts don't realize they are dead, and some do. I think that one of the points I do convey is that the choices and actions you make do not end after walking through death's door. I have witnessed strange things, and I have experienced occurrences that I still cannot explain to this day. What you are about to embark on as the reader is those "what if" scenarios that will only be answered when we finally make that fateful trip through death's door for ourselves. There are pieces of my life experiences in each and every one of my stories. Some of the stories will stand out as my favorites, and some will stand out as yours. My sincere hope for all that read these fictional; works is that you keep an open mind to the fact that death for many of these characters is not an end but a beginning.

That beginning is sometimes worse than the life they left behind. I have heard many times throughout my life when somebody dies that "Their pain is over." In these stories you will find out that it may not be true. I invite you all to take that trip into the afterlife with me and open your minds to what might hold true in the afterlife.

Daniel Norvell

PART I

For God and Country

For God and Country

I was 20 years old when that cannonball hit me in the chest. When I signed up, I never thought I would die in the war. I always hoped that I would someday meet President Lincoln and shake his hand. I respected the man and never gave a second thought to serving in the Union Army. I was Corporal Jeremiah Deakins, Union Soldier, and I vividly remember the day I died.

It was a warm, sunny fall afternoon. I was moving my men to another position on the battlefield when I lost my life. I heard the cannon blast just about the time the ball ripped a hole through my chest. Death came very quickly for me; I hardly had time to feel any pain. I remember lying on my back, and I turned my head to the side and gasped my last breath. As I stared into the eyes of one of my fallen men, I noticed a bright light on the hillside. Instantly, I was on my feet and walking toward this brilliant light with about 23 other men. I looked at the other men walking with me. There was much yelling and confusion, cannon fire, and gunfire all around us.

I remember looking back at my lifeless body and thinking, "Well, at least Momma will have something to bury."

I continued toward the light along with both Union and Reb soldiers. Most of the fellas walked right into that bright light, but one of the Rebs and I decided not to go. I have regretted that decision many times since; however, because of it, I've observed many things that I would never experience. The Reb looked at me, "Hey Yank, what the hell happened to us?"

"Well, Reb, I think we died. I think the war is over for you and me."

We sat on the hillside, that Reb and I, and watched the battle until it was over. There were many groans and a lot of smoke in the air. Death was all around us. More soldiers were walking toward the hillside, and they just seemed to disappear into nowhere. I never saw them again. Suddenly, that Reb jumped to his feet and took off running. He caught up with some of the men walking toward the hillside, and I never saw him again. I decided that I would make my way to our nation's capital. I had no idea what my existence would consist of, but I wanted to walk on the lawn of the White House and see our great President before I moved on to meet our Lord. I had no idea what I would see, but I felt the need to travel to Washington and at least gaze upon the face of the man I admired the most. I was not sorry I lost my life for my nation, and even if he couldn't hear me, I was going to tell President Lincoln that he had made the right choices. I would die for the man again if it were possible.

I walked for what seemed like weeks. I came into a clearing one night, and there was a lot of commotion with men shouting and screaming. I walked into this small group of men as they were placing a rope around the neck of a young Negro. The young man was terrified.

"Sir, please… I was hungry. I'll work to pay for the meat I took. I'm going home to my family. Please don't kill me!" His pleas fell on deaf ears. I ran into the group of men and tried to tell them to stop, but I couldn't do anything. They placed that man on a horse and tied the rope to a branch.

They called him a thief and said, "For your crimes, you're sentenced to death by hanging. May God have mercy on your soul." They slapped the horse, and, when it bolted, the young man's neck snapped, leaving him dangling and still twitching. I hit my knees and shook my head.

"Dear God, why? Why do men do such evil things to each other over the color of skin?" It was the first time I had ever seen a man hang, and I was sick to my stomach. I could not believe that I could still feel sickened by anything even though I was dead.

"I am sorry young man; I wish I could have stopped them."

I felt a hand on my shoulder, "I know you would have, soldier."

I turned and there, standing beside me, was the man these animals had just murdered.

"I was traveling home to see my mama. I found some ham that had fallen off a horse and was eating it when they rode up. They hung me for a piece of ham."

Feeling such remorse, all I could say was, "I'm sorry. I am so sorry. I lost my life trying to free your people."

With a smile on his face, the young man said, "It's okay, soldier. I must go now. Why don't you come with me?"

I looked into the man's eyes. "I cannot. I am going to Washington to gaze upon the President before I go anywhere else. I will get there before I go to be with our Lord." I wasn't sure why it was so important to me to go to Washington, but I was determined.

"Travel in peace, soldier. Thank you for your service to my people."

I looked around, and he was gone. All that was left was his body hanging from that tree. I sat down along the road with a heavy heart. I had just witnessed one of the cruelest acts ever, and it would not be the last.

As I continued my journey to the nation's capital, I passed a house early one morning and realized how nice it would be to smell a home-cooked meal. I made my way to the house and entered to smell bacon cooking. I sure missed food and a good horseback ride through the woods outside of the town where I lived. I was standing in the kitchen watching the woman of the house cook while her daughter helped. The man of the house came down from upstairs, and they sat and began to eat. I listened to the family talk, and it made me miss my own family. I should have traveled to see my mother instead of going to the capitol, but something drew me there. I couldn't explain it. There came a knock at the door, and the man of the house answered it, inviting the caller in. I heard the man call to his wife in a trembling voice. I heard a scream and followed the sound.

The woman of the house was on her knees, sobbing loudly, and her husband was consoling her. A Union captain was standing in the doorway. He had just advised them of their son's death in battle. I left them to mourn in peace, saying a prayer for the family as I went. I remembered that my mother had received similar news just months back, and I wished that I had reconsidered my choice of joining the army after what I had now observed. I thought of how my little brother and three sisters might have reacted when they got the news of my passing. My father was proud that I chose to serve, but I knew he was apprehensive at the same time. I would never know the pain of burying a son lost to battle, and I didn't envy my family for the pain my death had caused. I continued my journey with a heavy heart; I had been a young man with a long life ahead of me. I had promised to return and work for my father at his newspaper. I even left behind the girl I was to marry. What a fool I was to enter the war so blindly! I am proud to have served my country and my President, but I may have made a mistake. I spent the rest of that day, reminding myself of the injustice I had observed when those men hung that young man for no good reason, and the heaviness seemed to subside.

It was a few nights later that I had made my way into a small town that reminded me of home. The streets filled with people, and I knew that it must have been the Fourth of July. I made my way down the road and saw a man standing in the cemetery. He watched me as I walked by, but he never spoke a word. I felt uneasy as I passed, and I knew that I had just seen another dead man. He must not be able to leave his body in the cemetery, though I cannot imagine why. I was glad I had walked away from my body back on that battlefield, although I wondered where it ended up. I thought of the times I had spent as a boy with my friends at the swimming hole. But every time I think of that young man hanging from that tree, I do not regret the choice that I made.

I eventually came upon a house with a young man and woman sitting on the porch. He was talking with her, but I could not quite hear what they were saying. All at once, the woman stood up and smacked the young man across his face. The young man became furious, grabbed her by her hair, and dragged her to the back of the house. I followed them and saw that the man was on top of the woman. After he finished, he started to beat the woman in the face over and over. I ran over and tried to hit the man, but it was no use. The man kept beating this young woman until I heard gurgling, and I watched her take her last breaths. I was outraged. Why didn't anyone hear this and come to her aid?

There was celebrating going on, and that was the cover this coward needed to carry out his act. The young man ran off, and I followed. I was met at the gate by the man that was standing in the cemetery.

"Thank you for caring. I knew you would try to save my daughter, but I was sent here to bring her with me," he said.

"Daddy?" said a voice behind me. It was the young woman that I had just observed beaten to death. The man placed his arm around her, and they walked to the cemetery and disappeared. I returned to her lifeless body.

The young man had returned with the constable, "I saw him do it! I saw that negro beat her to death after he had his way with her!" I turned and walked away. I knew that another black man would hang. What made it even worse is that this man would hang for something he didn't do. I prayed to the Lord to take me.

"I am ready, Lord. I cannot continue to watch helplessly as these people die for being black."

I stayed in the town for about a week and unfortunately, I was right. After a quick trial, a young black man was hung for the crime of another man; there was no justice in the world. I hope that this injustice will not continue. It wasn't even a trial; it was a mockery of justice. I don't blame the court. I blame the liar that killed that girl and walked away without the truth ever being known. I walked away from the place I observed a second innocent black man die, and I noticed, for the first time, the man responsible for the crime was in uniform. He was a Union soldier! Again, I felt an empty feeling in my stomach. How could it be one of my men? He walked away, and I followed.

As he mounted his horse, I took a good look at his face. I would see him again, and I planned to be his judge, jury, and executioner. I followed this soldier for a few days until he reported back to his unit. Death came for him in battle. I observed the bullet rip through his face, and he laid on the ground, gasping. I walked over to the spot where he lay.

"It seems that your sin has caught up with you. You have dishonored that uniform and the right even to be considered a man."

The young man stared up at me in terror. I knew he could see me and hear me as he approached death's door. I sat back and watched as it took four hours for death to finally claim him. When it did, he stood and looked at me. "How did you know?"

"I was there the night you raped and beat that girl to death. I watched you allow an innocent man to hang for your crime. I pray that you be damned for your sins," I replied.

Before I could even finish that final sentence, a dark rider galloped toward us. He drew his sword and pierced the man through the chest. This man's soul was in torment and pain; I could see it. The dark horseman threw a rope around the man's neck and wrapped it around his saddle horn. The man's eyes widened, and there was a fire in them. The rider cracked its whip and dragged the man across the field, over the body that belonged to him, and disappeared into a black cloud. I wasn't sure, but I think I witnessed that man being dragged to Hell.

A few nights later, I was walking through a Union army encampment. The men were cleaning their guns and having a bite for dinner. There was a group of soldiers talking about what was going to happen in the morning. From what I could hear, two men were to be branded cowards. They had run from battle in the last skirmish, and that was the army's way of making sure the shame would follow them for the rest of their days. It made me feel better to be around the soldiers and remember the times I spent with my brothers around the fire. But I was not too comfortable with the fact that two young men were going to have the letter "C" branded onto their faces for the rest of their lives. I know that many men would have turned and run from their first battle.

As morning broke, the captain had the two men tied to big wooden poles in the middle of the camp. The fire blazed, and the branding irons were red hot in it. The captain stood and watched as the charges were read aloud, and the sentence was carried out. My God, they were just boys; not much older than 16, I thought. The first boy screamed in anguish and fainted when they branded him. The second boy wet his pants and cried. I could not believe the utter brutality of what I had witnessed. Those boys did nothing more than let their fear get the better of them, and they were branded for it. I had heard of the practice, but I had never witnessed it until then. Many of the men watching got sick. Some turned away and wept. I knew all would face death before facing torture such as this, and that is precisely the point the army was driving home by this act. It was still barbaric, and I never agreed with it. I walked away with a heavy feeling, in what was left of my very being, for those boys. This was not an act I would stand and witness again.

I walked for what seemed like a couple of days and ended up on a battlefield that reminded me of the one where my life ended. The battle had been over for a few hours, and the moaning and groaning had nearly stopped. I came upon a Rebel soldier holding his younger brother in his arms. The boy was dying. He had a gunshot wound to his stomach, and the older brother cradled him.

I watched as the younger brother gasped with his last breath, "John... John, an angel is standing here."

The boy stared directly at me and died with a little smile on his face. The older brother held the boy and cried. That's when I wondered if this war was worth fighting. I had seen more brutal acts after my death than I had witnessed in battle. These Rebs were no different from us. I did not agree with slavery at all, but it may not have been a reason for boys to kill each other on the field of battle either.

I walked away and kept my direction toward the capitol. I only wished I could tell the President of the acts I had witnessed since my death. I was confident he would be as sickened as I was. I walked on through the night, and the next day, I met the young man that had died in his brother's arms.

"I have been following you, angel. I want you to show me the way to heaven."

"I am no angel. I am also a soldier that died in battle. I witnessed you die, and I am sorry that you did; however, I cannot show you the way to heaven. I am not sure I will end up there," I responded.

The boy asked if he could walk with me for a while, and I welcomed the company of another. We talked, and I told him that even though we were on opposite sides, it no longer mattered because we now belonged to the afterlife. We walked into the night and came upon a house. A black man was standing outside, and there were three men on horseback talking with him.

"We aren't far from my home; I recognize that black man," the boy said. We approached and watched.

The black man was speaking to the three, "I am a free man. I have papers to prove that; you cannot search my house." Two of the men jumped off their horses.

One pointed a rifle at the black man, and the other entered the house. The black man turned to enter the house, and the man with the rifle growled, "You move another step, and I'll shoot you dead." In a couple of minutes, the other man emerged with a woman and two small children.

The man on horseback said, "You may be free, but them there are slaves. For harboring slaves, you die." Without another word, the man with the rifle shot the black man in the face. The woman screamed, and the boy that was with me ran to the fallen man's side.

"Why? Why did they shoot this man, angel?"

"I don't know. It is a senseless war."

The three men set his house on fire and rode off with the slaves. The boy knelt by the body for a long time.

"I would never have fought for the South if I would have known." I moved toward them and touched the boy's shoulder.

"I would not have fought for either side. Both sides are guilty of many crimes that go unknown. The only people that know the truth can no longer tell anyone; people like you and me."

"I never knew his name, angel. I only knew him because he used to walk by my family's farm to sell his wares in town. He was a good man." We sat there with the man until his house had smoldered to embers. "Angel... walk with me home. Walk with me to my family's farm." I agreed and said a prayer for the fallen man before we turned to leave. I only wished that I had a physical body to be able to give this man a proper burial.

We walked for a few hours and finally reached the farm of my traveling partner. He asked me to wait for him outside while he looked in on his family. While he was in the house, a dog walked up to me and started sniffing around my feet. I looked at the dog; he looked back at me and walked away. That dog knew I was there; he could see me. I then realized that animals could still see me in some form. The young man returned to the yard and told me he was going to stay around the farm and watch over his family.

He said he knew the Lord would come for him after he watched over them for a while. I wished him well and told him goodbye, and I continued my journey to the capitol.

I walked for what seemed to be days, and I could see a camp in the distance. I headed in the camp's direction and came upon another example of southern justice. Two men were beating up a young slave, kicking and hitting him in the chest and face. I yelled at them to stop and remembered that they couldn't hear me. I tried to think of anything I could do to change the almost inevitable outcome. One of the men went to his horse and grabbed a rope hanging on his saddle.

"Let's drag this bastard a while."

He tied the rope around the saddle horn and made a loop to place on the young man's leg. I went over to the horse and screamed at it as loud as I could. The horse lunged forward, and the rope tightened around the man's wrist before he could slip it onto the slave's leg. I clapped and yelled, "Giddy up!" and that horse took off with that cruel bastard dragging behind, screaming,

"STOP, STOP!" The other man jumped on his horse and took off in pursuit.

I walked over to the young slave and whispered in his ear, "If you can hear me, you had better get up and run."

Somehow, that boy must have heard me. He scrambled to his feet and took off running the opposite way. I may have saved that boy's life that night. Maybe that horse heard me, and perhaps he didn't, but that young man was alive. I hoped the horse would stop soon, but I did not regret making that horse run. I tried to follow the young slave, but I couldn't find him. I hoped that he would get away and make it to the North.

I continued to the camp and listened to the southern soldiers play some fiddle music. Even though they were supposed to be my enemy, they were no threat to me. I stayed at the camp until they had all fallen asleep for the night. I hoped it would not be much longer until I made it to the capitol.

I walked for a couple of days, and, in a tree, I found where the young slave had gotten to. His lifeless body hung from that tree. I felt total anguish for that man. Fate had assisted me in helping his escape two nights earlier only to meet the business end of the noose encircling his neck. I prayed for that man's soul. I felt disgusted by the fact that human life was considered worthless due to the color of skin. If it were possible, I would have cut this man down and buried him properly. Once more, I had to leave someone in a very disrespectful way because I couldn't do anything to change it. I knew that I had wandered for more than a year, although, at times, it seemed like just a few days. I was determined to make it to the capitol and gaze upon one of the men I held most dear.

I continued my travels and witnessed many more things that sickened me. I could think of nothing better than seeing the President and just standing in the same room, even if he couldn't see or hear me. I finally made it to Washington one night. I got my wish as I came face to face with President Lincoln, and it would be one of the saddest days of my existence. As I walked toward the White House, I was hoping to see the President and sit in the same room with him for a while. Traveling through our nation's capital, I came upon a crowd of people gathered around the house across the street from a theater. I hadn't seen that many people gathered in one place so quiet, it was almost as if they were silently waiting for something. They talked to each other but not much higher than a whisper; they all seemed so sad. I turned around and there, standing just outside of the theater, was the man I had traveled so far to see. President Lincoln walked toward the crowd as if he were looking for someone. He asked several questions to various people, but nobody would answer him.

"Mr. President," I said as I walked up to him.

With much surprise, the greatest man I'll ever meet responded, "Hello there, soldier, how are you tonight?"

"I am doing well, sir. It is my honor to meet you."

"Nice to meet you, son," The President responded. "The Mrs. and I were seeing a play in the theater over there, I got an excruciating headache, and I must have fallen asleep. I awoke to everyone gone from the theater, and I walked out here. You seem to be the only one that will talk to me."

"Mr. President, I would be honored to have a talk with you."

The President nodded. "Why don't you walk with me back to the White House? I seem to have lost my escorts, and you, being a soldier, can protect me."

"It will be my pleasure, Mr. President," I said.

24

We strolled toward the White House, and I told the President of the many things I had seen and encountered on my journey here. I explained to him that I was honored to serve in the army for his cause, but I was very apprehensive about the war.

"Well, son, there are times that decisions we have to make are the hardest ones in our lives, but we do the best we can, and that is all anyone can ask." We had finally made it to the White House, and I walked the President to the door. "Thank You for seeing me home, soldier. The guards will be relieved to see me returned unharmed due to your kindness."

"The honor was mine, Mr. President. I only wish that you would have had more time to see things through."

Puzzled, the President looked at me, and then he smiled and answered, "Well, son, re-elections can be won if we work hard enough at it." I smiled.

"Goodnight, sir, and God be with you and yours."

"Take care of yourself, son. Good night."

I walked away with a great feeling of pain in my soul. I knew that the President did not realize that he had died that night. I was not sure how it had happened, but the fact that he could talk to me and see me showed me that it was true. I did not have any idea how to tell him, so I decided not to. I hoped that he would find peace in his death, and I prayed for his soul and mine.

"Lord, please look after President Lincoln and his family. May he find peace in his afterlife." I had traveled for over a year to see that man, but when I finally did, it saddened me to know that he was also a victim of a senseless war. I decided to return to the home where I grew up and to be thankful for having no more of this tragedy in my existence. I finally made it home, and I recognized the smell of my mother's cooking immediately. I stayed around and watched my family. They would pray for me at dinner, and I later found out, while my parents were talking, that the President had fallen victim to a gunshot to his head. "So much pain; useless suffering," I thought to myself.

One night, I was drawn through the kitchen and outside of the house. Everyone was asleep, so I could not figure out what was going on. I walked outside of the house, and I heard a voice I had heard once before.

"Son, it is time to come home." There, before me, was President Lincoln.

"Mr. President, how did you find me?"

"The Lord sent me for you. He said you would come with me if I asked, so I am asking."

"What is it like, Mr. President? What is it like to be with the Lord?"

The President replied, "It is different for us all, son, but your days of wandering are over. Someday your parents will join you there, but, for now, we have much to talk about." I walked across my parent's lawn with one of the greatest men that had ever lived. I made sure that he made it home the night of his death, and he had now come to return the gesture.

PART II

Jayme's Diary

DAN NORVELL

Chapter 1

Meeting a Boy

I couldn't believe that Alan asked me out. I always considered myself a bookworm, and I hadn't gone out with too many guys before. He asked if I could meet him at the school tomorrow night so we could exchange phone numbers, and I could give him my address so he could pick me up Friday night. I walked home from school that day on cloud nine. I thought Alan was so cute, and he was such a nice guy.

When I got home, my mom was still at work. I couldn't wait to tell her about Alan. She was always telling me that I needed to get out with friends and quit staring at the walls and doing homework so much. I was still a Junior in high school; she thought I should go out and see what dating and hanging out with friends was like. I never really had any friends since coming to this new town, my dad had passed away from cancer, and Mom and I moved here for a fresh start. I couldn't wait to be able to tell her about it all.

I went into my room, and I pulled my diary out from underneath my bed and wrote a quick entry:

September 12, 2010 - Alan asked me out to dinner and a movie. Can't wait!

I wrote everything in that diary, and this was a big day for me. We had only been here for six months, and I barely finished the last school year. It was a good thing I have always been an honor roll student, or I probably wouldn't have been a Junior this year. I told my mom everything when she got home that night. She hugged me and told me that she knew we would fit in here. I went to sleep that night the happiest I had been since we had lost my father last year. We had only been back at school for three weeks, and it was already shaping up to be a good year. Before I went to bed that night, I added to my previous entry in my diary:

I am looking forward to seeing Alan tomorrow night. He is such a nice guy, and this date is what I needed for a new start. I think it's good for Mom and me both.

I went to school the next morning, and it was hard to concentrate on the day. I could only think of Alan meeting me tonight. I passed him in the hallway between classes, and he smiled at me.

I saw him again just before school got out for the day, and he came up to me, "I'll see ya later tonight, Jayme." I just smiled and nodded my head. Alan leaned in and kissed me on the cheek; I smiled and started to feel my face get hot. Everyone had seen Alan kiss my cheek, and I wanted to melt right then and there. I smiled, and he walked away. He looked back at me twice, and I knew we would have a great time together on our date.

I ran all the way home and finished my homework in record time that night. I grabbed my diary from under the bed:

September 13, 2010 - *I meet with Alan tonight! Can't wait, he's so cute!*

I made a sandwich and left Mom a note to tell her I would see her when I got home after meeting with Alan. I grabbed my jacket and ran out the door toward school; I knew Alan would be there soon.

I arrived at the school and sat on the front steps and waited for Alan to arrive. It was starting to get dark, and he still was not there yet. I waited for another hour, and still no Alan. I was heartbroken.

How could he do this to me? By the time I started walking home, tears were streaming down my face. A car pulled up beside me, and there were three guys from school in it. They were all seniors, and I recognized two of them by face, but not by name. I knew the boy in the passenger seat of the car. It was Jake. I didn't know his last name, but he was a jock, and he and his friends were pretty stuck up. The car slowed to a stop.

"Jayme? That's your name, isn't it? Are you okay? Do you need a ride?" Jake asked.

"No Thanks. I just need to walk. Thank you, though."

The car stopped by the park, about halfway between my house and the school. All three of the boys got out of the car and walked up to me.

Jake stood in front of me, "Jayme, I think you should take a ride with us, you look upset, and I don't want you to be alone when I know you are upset."

"No, Jake... I'm okay. My mom is expecting me home in a minute. I really need to go." I replied.

"No, you don't!" Jake said as he grabbed my arm. They all grabbed me and threw me into the back seat of the car.

"What are you doing!?!" I screamed, "Jake! Let me go! I have to get home!"

"You aren't going anywhere! Let's get out of town, John!" Jake told the boy that was driving. Jake and the other boy held me in the back seat of the car, while John, the boy in the driver's seat, drove quickly out of town. They drove for about 20 minutes, and the whole time I pleaded with them to take me back home. The car finally stopped. They turned the car off and pulled me out. One of the boys started to try and pull my pants off. When I began to scream, Jake punched me in the face. I could feel the blood start to pour from my mouth as I began to cry.

"Jake, please. Please stop. I won't tell anybody if you just stop."

"Shut up, you stuck up bitch!" Jake said as he punched me again.

I could feel my eye start to swell shut as the boys wrestled me to the ground. I could feel them trying to pull my pants off again, and I tried to wiggle around and fight as hard as I could.

I heard Jake say to one of the boys, "Give me that rock!" I felt a sharp pain on the side of my head, and everything went completely black. I woke up outside of the school to find there was nobody around. As I started to walk home, I began crying and knew my mom would be furious when I told her about what those boys had tried to do to me.

The house was completely dark when I finally made it home. I walked in and yelled, "Mom! Mom, where are you? Mom, I need to talk to you. Something happened tonight." I looked around the house, and I couldn't find her anywhere. I went into my room, noticed it was 1:00 a.m., and I grabbed my diary under the bed:

September 14, 2010 - Jake Edwards and his friends pulled me into a car and drove me to the country. They beat me up and tried to attack me. They must have knocked me out because I woke up at the school.

That was all I felt like writing. I was going to wait right here until my mom returned. She was probably out looking for me. I laid down on my bed, and I was thinking about how odd it was that I could not feel how bad my face should have hurt considering how hard Jake had punched me in it. Feeling tired, I started to fall asleep. As I looked out into the hallway of the darkened house, a light was visible. It was a bright light, and I could hear my father's voice. I sprang from the bed and walked out into the hallway.

"Daddy? Daddy, is that you?"

"Jayme. Come to the light, honey. I am here waiting for you. Come here, sweetheart, Daddy is here waiting for you."

I started toward the light, and just then, I heard keys in the door. I stopped and spun around. The light in the hallway disappeared as the light in the kitchen came on. My mom walked into the house, and she looked worried. She threw her car keys onto the table, and she started to cry. I was making my way to her when the phone rang. I heard my mom say, "Oh my God," she picked up her keys and ran out of the house. I didn't even have time to say anything to her. I just turned around and walked back into my bedroom. I would just talk to her in the morning.

Chapter 2

Why Won't Any of you Listen?

I must have slept for hours. I woke up and walked around the house to find my mom had returned, and she was asleep on the couch. There was an empty bottle of rum next to her. It's been years since my mother last drank, I knew she and Daddy drank when they went out but never like this, and never a whole bottle.

Breaking the silence, a knock on the front door woke my mother from her sleep. Getting off the couch, she greeted some policemen standing outside the door. I could hear whispers and saw what looked like a priest standing with the police. My mother started to scream as the priest grabbed her as she sobbed. They all walked into the living room and sat down as my mother continued to sob uncontrollably.

As the police asked her questions, I heard my mother say, "The boy's name was Alan. She said he goes to school with her. That is all I know."

I walked into the room, and I said, "It was Jake Edwards that beat me up, Mom. He and his friends. One of them was named John." Nobody even paid any attention to me or to what I was saying. "Mom! I said it was Jake Edwards! Why won't any of you listen?" Everything I said fell on deaf ears. My own mother would not even peel herself away to come and hug me, and see if I was okay. I decided to go and write the whole thing down in my diary.

September 14, 2010 - Last night, I went to meet with Alan. Jake Edwards and two of his friends came up to me and pulled me into their car. They drove for around 20 minutes, and then they stopped on some road and beat me up. Alan had nothing to do with it; I didn't even see him last night. I can't understand why nobody will listen to me!

My mother got dressed and left with the police and the priest. I was so upset about being ignored; I just stayed in my room for the rest of the day. To pass the time, I decided to put my clothes away and listen to some music until she returned. Maybe she would want to talk then. Hours had passed, and finally, I could hear keys in the front door. My mother entered the house, my aunt Beth, and my cousin Sarah quietly came in behind her. I found it very strange that Mom had not told me that they were coming. They all were so quiet and looked as if they had been crying for a long time.

"Beth, I can't handle this anymore today. I have to take some aspirin and lay down."

"That's okay, Tina. If you need us, Sarah and I will be right here." Beth hugged my mother, and I walked out to greet them all.

"When did you guys get here?" I asked. Nobody answered.

"Sarah, I haven't seen you since Daddy's funeral. How are you?"

Sarah just stared off into space. I just sat down in a chair and shook my head, what is going on with everyone? They should be happy. I am here and okay, but nobody will speak to me. I got upset, and I went back to my room and grabbed my diary.

September 14, 2010 - My aunt Beth and cousin Sarah got here today. I don't know why they are here, but they won't even talk to me. Did I do something wrong here? Mom won't even speak to me. Their ignoring me had better end soon, I am the one that gets beat up and attacked by Jake and those other boys, and I get treated like the outcast.

34

I laid down on my bed, and I must have fallen asleep. When I woke up, I decided to get up, get dressed, and go outside. It looked like the sun was shining, and I didn't even leave the house yesterday. I put on my clothes, and I went down to the kitchen to find no one was home. How late did I sleep? My mom, my aunt, and cousin were all gone. I could not believe that they were treating me this way. I walked outside, and there were candles all over the sidewalk in front of my house. There were ribbons tied around the trees, and cards stapled to the fence.

"What in the heck is going on here?" I thought. I walked out and started reading the cards; I couldn't believe what I was reading. The cards were all from kids at my school. They all had writing in them about how much I would be missed, and how sorry they were that some of them hadn't gotten a chance to know me. I was so confused, but maybe I could get answers at school.

Walking up to the front of the school, I saw two policemen were bringing Alan out in handcuffs. He was telling them that he had not even seen me that night. The one officer told him to shut up, and he could make a statement at the police station when his parents got there. Why in the heck were they arresting Alan? What did he do? What did it have to do with me? I watched as the police car pulled away from the school with Alan in the back. When I walked into the school, none of the students inside said a word. The halls were completely silent as people walked back and forth to their classes. When I reached my locker, I found more ribbons and cards plastered all over the door of it.

Not until I saw the card that said, "R.I.P. Jayme, we love you," did I finally figure out what had happened. Jake and his friends had beaten me to death. That had to be the answer. It was the only one that made sense. I suddenly remembered the light in the hallway, my dad's voice, everyone ignoring me; it was all happening because they could not see me. I felt so alone. I could not even believe what had happened. The worst part about it all was they arrested Alan thinking it was him that beat me to death while Jake and the other two were free. I didn't know what to do. I can't believe how helpless I felt. I started to think about my poor mom. She and I had just buried my dad not even a year ago, and now she had to bury me.

Running out of the school, I turned towards home. My mother was sitting on the couch, and she was crying again. My aunt Beth was seated beside her, and Sarah was on the other side, holding her hand. I heard my aunt Beth say that Grandma would be here soon, and so would my uncle Brian. I was happy to know that my mom would have family around her, but I wished that I could walk up and hug her and tell her I was here with her. I felt so many emotions. I was angry for being taken from my mother, I was sad for my mother, and I wanted to see the boys that were truly guilty for this crime go to jail for it, not Alan. I was upset he hadn't come to meet me, and maybe if he had not stood me up, I would be alive right now. I couldn't blame Alan though, even if he hadn't shown up, he was not the one that murdered me.

The next few days were exhausting on my mother. She would lay in my room, on my bed, and hold my stuffed tiger she and my father had bought me when I was little. She would smell my pillow and start to cry. I would sit beside her, and I would try to hold her hand, but she could not feel me there. I was surprised at how much anguish I felt when I attended my own funeral. I think every student and teacher from our school was there. They would go up to the front of the church and stare at me lying there. The other girls would start to cry, and the teachers would just walk away, shaking their heads. As the priest began the funeral mass, I walked up and gazed at my face. It was swollen and didn't even look like me at all. I could not believe that the last time my mother saw my face, this is what she would remember. It was sickening and unfair.

I stood there in the church, and I watched as the people sat and listened to the priest talk. I could hear my mother wail out in anguish as they closed my casket for the last time. When they left the church, I followed them to the cemetery. They were going to put up a false stone here so that the students could come to visit it to remember me. My mother would have me buried back where they buried my father. After the service, I went home and pulled the diary out from under my bed:

September 20, 2010 - *I attended my own funeral today. I watched as people from my school that I never knew cried and said goodbye. I did not notice Jake Edwards or the other two boys that killed me there. I guess they could not face that people missed me* *and what they had really done to more people than just me. I hope that someday the police figure out that Alan is innocent, and Jake Edwards and his friends are the ones that killed me. The fact that Alan is now sitting in jail for my murder makes this twice as tragic.*

It would be the last entry I would ever make in my diary.

DAN NORVELL

Chapter 3

Your Life was a Miracle

I had been sitting around the house for over a month now. I watched as my mother sunk into a deep depression. I was worried about her, but there wasn't anything I could do. My aunt Beth and Cousin Sarah had returned home two weeks ago, and my grandmother was still here with my mother. When I walked into the kitchen, she was sitting there, lighting a cigarette. She hadn't smoked since I was little. My grandmother walked in and sat down across the table from my mother.

"I know how difficult this has been on you, sweetheart, but you cannot keep blaming yourself," my grandmother told her.

"Who do I blame Mom? If I hadn't told her she could go meet that boy, she would be walking around here with me right now. She was all I had left to live for," My mother said as she began to break down and cry.

My grandmother got up from her chair, walked around the table, and grabbed my mother in her arms, "It is not your fault. Your sister, your brother, and I are still here; we are here to live for."

"I want to die, Mom! I want to have the Lord take me now! I cannot think of living anymore without her!"

I ran out of the kitchen and to my room. I could not stand to hear my mother speak this way. I just wished I had not ever met Alan, or left the house that night. I was sitting in my room, and I heard a voice from behind me, "Jayme, it isn't your fault. If it was meant to be, it was meant to be."

I recognized the voice immediately, "Daddy? What are you doing here?" I asked as I ran to hug him.

He hugged me back, "I came to tell you what you need to do, Jayme. Alan is innocent, and your mother will be joining us here of we don't help her. You cannot come with me until we help your mom."

"What can we do to help her, Daddy? After you died, she almost died with you. I was all she had left."

"That isn't true, sweetheart. She has her mother, and Beth, and Brian. Your grandma will need your mom soon. Your mom needs to get through this."

"What do I need to do, Daddy?"

"Go to your mom in her sleep. Tell her you are okay, and that you are with me. Tell her you will never be far from her. Most importantly, tell her to find your diary. It will prove Alan is innocent."

I followed my father's instructions. That night when my mother fell asleep, I slipped into her room and whispered into her ear. As I spoke to her, she moved around and became restless.

She screamed out, "JAYME! Jayme, where are you?!" My mother just started to freak out and throw pillows, and grabbing things off her dresser, and flinging them across her room. I backed up and began to cry.

I could feel my father's arms around me, "It's okay, honey. She will get through this; she just needs to get her anger out. We have to keep trying. We have to try until she finds that diary."

"I'll keep trying Daddy, but it makes me so sad to see Mom like this."

"I know it does sweetheart, but we have to do it."

I kept trying for weeks. I would whisper in my mother's ear at night, and she would either ignore me, or she would freak out. One night I was getting ready to speak to my mom; I went to her bedroom, and she wasn't there. I started looking all over the house for her, but I couldn't find her anywhere. I started back toward my room, and I heard a thud in the bathroom. I walked through the door to see my mother had cut her wrists and sat bleeding all over the floor.

I started to scream, "Grandma! Grandma!!! Come to the bathroom!" I heard footsteps coming down the hallway, my grandmother entered the room, and she let out a shriek.

"My God! Hold on honey, I'll call an ambulance!"

My grandmother ran out of the room, and I could hear her panicked voice on the phone to the 911 operator. I got down close to my mom, and I looked her in the eyes, "Why Mom? Why did you do this to yourself?"

"I can't live without you," she answered me.

"Mom? You can hear me?"

I heard my father behind me, "Tell her everything right now, Jayme. She can hear you clearly."

I told her, "Mom, you can't die and leave grandma; she needs you. I'll always be here with you, mom. Tell Grandma to get my diary and bring it to you. I love you, mom. Bye."

"Don't leave Jayme! I can't live anymore without you. I can see your eyes right now; I can't think about not seeing them again, don't leave me here."

My mother could see me. "Mom, I don't have long. Alan didn't kill me, a boy named Jake Edwards and his friends did. It's in my diary. I'll always be with you, mom. Always. I love you!"

The paramedics arrived, and they started to treat my mom. I heard her ask my grandmother to find my diary, but my grandmother would not listen. She followed the paramedics out of the house, and my father and I were left there alone.

"Daddy? Do you think she'll be okay?"

"She is going to be fine now, Jayme. She'll be just fine now. It's time to go."

My dad held his hand out, and I took it. A light appeared at the end of the hallway, and my father and I walked through it.

I look in on my mother from time to time; she finally did get my diary and convinced one detective to check things out. One of the boys that were there when Jake killed me could not keep quiet anymore, and he told the detective everything. They had planned on getting their kicks with me and leaving me out on that road. Their intent was never murder, though it seemed like Jake had other plans. When they interview him, Jake told the police he knew a dead person couldn't testify against him.

Alan was released, and he and his family visit my memorial gravestone every year and place flowers on it.

I was standing in the cemetery one day, and I heard Alan tell his mother, "If it hadn't been for Jayme's mother finding her diary, I would have been in prison for something I didn't do." Every time Alan visited the cemetery, he always kissed his hand and placed it on the stone. He always said, "Thank You, Jayme. Thank You for never giving up, even after you were gone."

My mother got better, and she started a foundation for other parents that have lost children to violence and bullying by their peers. Every time I check on her, I visit her in her dreams. I tell her how proud I am of her, and that I will always be with her.

She would look at me and say, "Do you really have to leave? You just got here. I miss you." I always tell her, "I miss you too, mom, but you have people to help, and you need to show them my diary. The diary that proves to them that their kids are with them too."

She always tells me, "Your life was a miracle, Jayme."

I always reply to her, "Yours is, mom. Your life and my diary are the miracles."

PART III

A Ghost's Account

DAN NORVELL

Chapter 1

A Ghost's Account

It was a cold day in January. I remember the paramedics asking how many pills I took as I lay there on the gurney. And that siren was blaring… blaring… BLARING! The next memory I had was sitting at the dinner table with my wife. She wouldn't look at me or acknowledge my presence. She just sat there staring through me, asking why. I tried to tell her; I tried explaining that the pain was too great; that I couldn't cope without the medication the doctors had given me. I couldn't seem to take enough to numb the pain any longer. And I was getting tired of answering her and getting nothing more than a blank stare.

For at least two years, I lived in this house with her in complete silence. I tried to talk to her, but she would either just walk away or go out for a drive until, one day, she didn't return. I couldn't imagine what I had done to deserve her actions. I just sat and stared out the window. The house seemed so still. I reflected on what it could have been that drove her from me. I stared out into the back yard on a warm summer day, when a couple of kids walked across my lawn… MY lawn. I hadn't mowed it in quite a while; it was long and really needed it. I yelled at them to get out of my yard, but it seemed my screams fell on deaf ears. Those boys were so disrespectful. Who did they think they were?

One night as I lay in bed, wide awake, I heard a noise in the kitchen. The house was tranquil and still, as it often was lately, and I got out of bed to look around and make sure my home was secure. If those boys had returned to mess with my house for me yelling at them, well, they were going to get an earful. How dare someone enter my house, in the middle of the night, to repay me for yelling at them. I walked through the house, and I found nothing. Nothing was there. I called out… to nothing.

I went back to bed, and I was restless. I needed my pills, where were they? I looked all over for those pills; I couldn't find them anywhere. "What's the use?" I remember thinking. Why did those paramedics waste their time years ago? What kind of life was I living anyhow? I sat all day and night, I couldn't remember meals or craving a drink of water. Nothing seemed to matter. But why was I destined to be stuck in the depression my wife left behind the day she drove off and left without a word?

It was late winter when I heard the door open in the house. I walked into my living room to what appeared to be a young couple, looking toward me like I had no right in my own home. Those kids moved in without a word, just walked right in like they owned the place! When did I lose my voice? Why am I not being heard? What am I supposed to do to make these people get the message?

Chapter 2

The Next Account

How was I going to tell these kids nicely to get the hell out of my house? They moved in like I wasn't even here. They ignored everything I said and then started to rip apart my kitchen! Nights are running into days, and days are running into nights. I was so confused. I still couldn't find my pills.

The last time I remember talking to anyone was a week before I went to the hospital. I spoke with my priest and explained to him that the pain in my back had become unbearable. The funny thing is that ever since the trip to the hospital, I couldn't remember any pain, but I craved the pills anyway. I often thought back to that hospital trip. Why couldn't I remember coming back home? When did the doctor release me? Why hadn't any of my friends come to visit?

The only thing that gave me any solace was the radio I listened to in the middle of the night. My wife used to get upset at me for listening to it at all hours, and the new lady of the house does the same. She paraded in and turned it off every time I turned it on. She reminded me of my wife, and it upset me that things ended the way they did between us. I just felt that I couldn't get my point across to anyone in the past few months. I needed to see a doctor and find out if I was crazy.

I saw and heard things I couldn't explain. I was having a difficult time remembering the last time I had a meal, but I never seemed to be hungry. I wished I could return to a simpler time, when things made sense, when my wife and I could take on the world together. We built so many memories in this house. How could she just leave? Without a word, she just got up and left.

Chapter 3

I Must Be Crazy!

I was sitting in my living room staring out the window, thinking of how perfect my life once was. I heard some sort of a ruckus coming from the lady in the bedroom. She was screaming, and I went in to investigate. I looked around the doorway, and the lady of the house was sitting in a pool of blood as her husband was on the phone yelling, "Just get here... get here as fast as you can!" The ambulance pulled up, and they took the lady away. I'm still not sure what happened. I remember seeing her about a week later, she was sitting in the room the couple referred to as the nursery, crying. She kept a daily routine in the nursery for about a month. Then the nursery disappeared under boxes and packing material. One day, as quickly as they appeared, the young couple was gone. The house was empty and still, but I couldn't believe my luck... they had left the radio.

I turned it on and let it play for hours that night. I remember the young couple, and even though they frustrated me, I liked them. The house just seemed so empty. I remember the lady of the house cooking and singing lullabies like the ones many of my friends' wives hummed when they were expecting. I wondered where they went.

The electricity in the house went off one day, and I could no longer listen to my radio. Even though I couldn't remember writing the check, I was sure I paid the electric bill. I also found it very odd that, even though it was snowing outside, I never felt cold even though the electricity had been off in the house for months. What the hell was happening?

I have felt empty and alone since the young couple moved. Once again, I was left without a word. No explanation, no thanks for letting us stay here, nothing. Two more winters passed, and then one day, there was a man standing in the doorway of my living room. He was wearing a suit, and I knew he was there to cause me trouble, I could feel it.

He looked over at me sitting on the couch the young couple had left there, and he never spoke one word. He looked around as if he owned the place, and this disgusting grin crossed his face. "It's perfect," he muttered under his breath. I don't know what made me feel this way, but I had a gut feeling that this was one of the most heartless individuals I had ever seen. I actually felt uneasy and almost scared. I am not quite sure what his intent is, but I am hoping he ignores me as the young couple did. If he stays clear of me, I will stay clear of him; unless he takes my radio. Then we may have an issue.

Chapter 4

True Evil

It was late spring, I think, when the man in the suit moved his family into my house. It was the man, his wife, and their two little kids. The little boy looked to be about 6 years old, and the little girl appeared to be about 8. I never heard anyone but this loudmouth day in and day out. He yakked on the phone all day long and then went to work on the second shift. He returned home drunk, and then I heard the smacks coming from the room that he and his wife occupied. Then he made a nightly stop in his daughter's room. Most times, he didn't come out until the morning. There was something not right with this guy, something that made me shudder. I wanted to say something, but it wasn't my place. Or was it? I mean, this was my house, and they were guests here—uninvited guests. This behavior was an everyday occurrence until one fall weekend.

It was a Friday night. I remember it was Friday because I heard the loudmouth say that he had plans for the weekend. I heard him tell his wife, "you better not mess the weekend up for me, or I'll beat the shit out of you, you worthless bitch." I was so mad that I entertained the thought of hitting him. Instead, I told him to shut his mouth and not speak that way to her in my house. He ignored me, of course. The whole family did, and I had become used to that treatment.

Later that night, the bastard came home and went into the bedroom he shared with his wife. I heard the smacks, and I could smell the liquor on him when he walked into the house. He was a drunken mess. He was shouting and cursing, and the kids were crying. I heard the lady of the house yell to him, "if you touch her again, I swear to God, I'll kill you." His reply was, "you and whose army, you bitch. You couldn't stop a toilet from overflowing." I heard him make his way across the room as I started for the stairs. His feet were heavy, and his venomous words cut into my very soul. How could a father and husband treat his wife and kids in this manner?

I was going to burst into that bedroom and beat the hell out of this guy because I knew the reason for his nightly visits to his daughter's room. As I reached for the doorknob, I heard a shot ring out; then three more. I heard one final shot as I crossed the threshold, and I could hear the children screaming in their rooms. The lady had made good on her promise; she had shot him right between his eyes. She made sure he was dead by shooting him once in his crotch and twice through his chest. There was blood everywhere. She stood there, trembling, and looked directly at me.

"Who are you?" she asked.

"I am the owner of this house," I responded.

I told her to put the gun down. As she dropped the gun, I saw the light behind her. The light was so brilliant and peaceful. She turned and walked into it and, as quickly as it appeared, it was gone.

The only things left in that room were two bodies, the woman and her husband. The last shot I heard was the one that ended her life. What did I just witness? How did she talk to me when she was already dead? Where were those kids? I turned, and there stood the children, sobbing. My heart had never felt so heavy before or since. I felt so sorry for those children. I can't even imagine what they were feeling. I went to them and knelt down to their level.

"Don't look; it is nothing you need to see. Let's go downstairs and wait for the police," I said to coax them from the horrific scene.

They turned and, without another word, we walked downstairs and waited for the police to arrive.

The police called a grandmother and, for the third time in a few years, the house was empty again. That terrible night haunted my memory every day. I couldn't close my eyes without remembering the look on that woman's face as she spoke to me for the first and last time. She was the first person that acknowledged me in years, and she was dead when she did it.

DAN NORVELL

Chapter 5

Evil Returns

The house sat still and empty for many months. People would stop and look around the house. I could hear bits of muffled discussion in the kitchen or the living room; then they would leave. I remember thinking that I hadn't invited these people. Why did they come to my house, walk around my kitchen and living room, and never even ask me if it was OK? I cannot believe how ignorant people can be. They came into my house, lived their lives, and then, as quickly as they arrived, they left.

It was about nine months later when the blinds were opened, and the new occupants that would share my house started moving in. They were two brothers. One had spent some time in the service and was wounded in the war. The other was a businessperson of some kind. I remember the soldier had terrible nightmares of his time spent in Iraq. He would wake up with cold sweats and head for the shower.

It was one night in late fall when the soldier asked his brother if he had heard or felt anything strange in the house. I had never heard anything odd in the house, and I had been here for years. I could hear only bits and pieces of the conversation, but it was clear the soldier was scared. He was scared to death of the man he said he saw behind him in the mirror when he shaved. He said the man whispered into his ear at night while he tried to sleep. I remember thinking that I was the only other man in this house, and I hadn't said a word to either of the brothers.

I respected the soldier for his service to our country. How he got hurt in Iraq was beyond me because that war had ended already. So, who were they speaking of? I was intrigued and alarmed. I walked closer to the brothers so I could hear the conversation more clearly.

"I don't know who it is, Jerry, but this fricken' guy is pissed," the soldier said.

"Jack, you have been through a lot. We will call the doctor tomorrow. I promised Mom before she died that I would take care of you, and I will little brother," the elder brother said, reassuringly.

Jack was trembling. The color drained from his face as he described the heaviness he felt in the house at night. He described the pushes he would feel as he would walk into the bedroom where "it happened." I tried, in vain, to reassure Jack as well, "Calm down, kid. The war is over for you." I had served in Iraq. That is where I had gotten my back injury and why the pain pills were prescribed. I knew his pain, and I knew the stress and thoughts and feelings that followed when we returned home.

"That pedophile prick is here, Jerry. His wife shot him, and he stayed behind," Jack told his brother. I could see why Jack would be uncomfortable, but I hadn't seen or felt anything. I wasn't sure what Jack was talking about, but I would later find out. Over the next few months, I started to hear a familiar voice, the same angry voice I thought had been silenced by bullets. For God's sake, was Jack right? Was this guy still here in some form? How were we going to get him out of here? What were we going to do to keep this evil piece of garbage at bay?

It was one night in the living room, and Jack had fallen into a restless sleep. I sat in the living room with him as he watched TV and finally nodded off. Then I heard it. I heard the voice of the man that had committed one of the worst acts a person could commit. I thought he had left, but here he was. I could see him.

He leaned over Jack and whispered into his ear. "Soldier boy… soldier boy… SOLDIER BOY!"

Jack sat up and looked around. The man was gone as quickly as he appeared. I looked at Jack and said, "I believe you now, kid."

I knew that I had, in fact, just looked at the ghost of the evilest, empty person I have ever seen. I know that whatever he is, he is now messing with this kid because he can no longer inflict physical pain on his own children. I remember yelling out, "Leave him alone, you rotten son of a bitch!" All I heard was an evil chuckle. What in the hell was going on here?

Chapter 6

Evil Makes His Move

Jack was at the end of his rope. This guy took joy in really making Jack's life miserable. I had only seen him once, but that was all it took for me to believe Jack. Jerry called the doctor one night while I listened in the kitchen. He thought Jack was suffering from something they call PTSD. I wasn't sure what it was, but I was sure Jack suffered from the continuous tirade of crap this guy whispered into his ear every night. I stood in Jack's room every night and watched. When he slept on the couch, the man started his abuse. When he slept in his room, the man started his abuse. It was really starting to piss me off. This kid served God and country, and this baby-raping garbage heap found pleasure in elevating his pain.

Jack was driven to the brink the second time I saw the man. Jack locked himself in the bathroom, and Jerry called the ambulance. Jack was screaming, "stay out of my head!" I felt so sorry for this kid because he was helpless. I felt helpless, too. How do you fight what you can't see? By the time the paramedics arrived, Jack's wailing had stopped. Jerry and the paramedics pushed the door open to find Jack on the floor in a growing pool of blood. Jack had taken a razor and slit his wrists so deep that I thought he had died for sure.

The paramedics rushed him out of the house while I stood in the bathroom in shock. I thought of all the tragedy this house had seen over the years, and how much of it I had observed with my own eyes. As I stood there, I noticed the fogged mirror. On it was written, "Soldier boy Jack, why did you ever come back?"

I shouted out, "Why don't you try that shit with me, you dark son of a bitch!" I punched the mirror as hard as I could. I hit that mirror at least five times, but the message was still there, fading only as the cool air filled the bathroom. I caught a glimpse of a shadow standing behind the shower curtain, and then it was gone.

Jack was gone for weeks; I missed that kid. He was a kindred spirit, a soldier who reminded me of myself. I sat in the living room and watched out the window. Every time the car pulled up, I expected Jerry to help Jack into the house. It never happened. One night, Jerry came home and started packing Jack's things. I later heard him on the phone, thanking the doctor for everything he had done. The last thing Jerry packed into the box was a picture of Jack in his uniform.

"I am so sorry, Jack. I failed you. And mom, I failed you, too!"

Jerry sobbed loudly into his hands, falling to his knees. I asked Jerry what happened, and he didn't answer. My worst feelings were confirmed a few days later when Jerry carried in the flag that had been draped over his little brother's casket. The thing was, the whole time Jack was gone, I never heard or saw anything in the house. I looked every night for that sick bastard and never found him. He never made himself known to anyone, but Jack and me. Now, Jack was gone, and I knew this man was responsible in some way.

About a month later, an event I had become used to came to pass once more. The boxes came in, Jerry packed them up and moved away. I never saw him again. I missed Jerry and Jack, and I felt terrible for that kid. I walked into the room Jack had stayed in while he lived here, and for the first time in years, I dropped to my knees and prayed. I prayed Jack would find peace, and I prayed that if hell existed, the man in the suit would be condemned to it.

Chapter 7

The End of Innocence

It was late summer. A few months after Jerry left my house, the most angelic little girl I had ever seen moved in with her parents. I saw her walk up the sidewalk outside and heard her little voice as she said, "Mommy, is this my room?" I cringed with fear. I told the little girl's mommy that maybe that would not be a good room for her, but she just gave me the same blank stare that I always got. A month after they settled in, the torture of this little girl began.

It began as the boogie man in the closet story. The little girl would run into her parents' room, and they would tell her there's no such thing as ghosts or a boogie man. I remember thinking they were right; this man was worse. The little girl became the object of the man's twisted desires. She woke up crying every night. I finally got so sick of it that, one day, while the family was gone, I walked around the house screaming at the top of my lungs, "Why? Why don't you go and rot in hell? It wasn't enough that you tortured your own child and Jack. I hope that hell has a burner for your ass, you sick son of a bitch!" I never got a response. I finally started sleeping in little Shelly's room every night, but I never saw or heard anything. I watched her until she woke up screaming. I was never aware of any presence.

One morning, Shelly woke up with scratch marks all over her stomach. Her mother was horrified. She asked what had happened, and Shelly said the boogie man was touching her. I was beyond pissed. I planned to make it my mission to banish this sick bastard to hell. I prayed to God every night to give me one shot at this prick. I prayed that God would give me the ability to hogtie this guy and throw him into the pit of hell. One night, I lay in the living room looking out the window, thinking of the hell I've endured watching the suffering in this house. I was just about to walk upstairs when I heard Shelly's terrified scream. I charged up the stairs, two at a time, and into her room. I saw that beautiful little face with three deep scratches across it.

I was at my wit's end. "That's it!" I shouted.

"Where are you? Where are you, you cowardly baby-raper? Why don't you come and face me?" I got my wish. There he was, standing in Shelly's closet, the bullet hole between his eyes.

"I have heard you all this time. I just refuse to listen to a reject," he muttered.

I walked up to him and said, "Death was too good for you, you sick bastard! Why don't you go to hell where the pieces of shit like you should be flushed!"

"You haven't got the balls for it," he replied with a cold smile. He backed into the closet and disappeared. I ran into the closet and pounded on the wall.

"They should have ground your nuts in a blender before they buried you, you sick prick! You stay away from that girl! You stay away from Shelly!"

After that confrontation, things were quiet for around a month. That is when Paige came into the picture. Paige was the family's answer to the attacks on Shelly. Paige proved to be a guardian angel sent from above for both Shelly and me.

Chapter 8

The Battle Begins

Paige came into Shelly's room and introduced herself. "I'm Paige, and I am going to make the boogie man go away." Shelly got off of her bed and hugged Paige with tears streaming down her face. "Thank you," she whispered. Paige asked Shelly to leave the room and go downstairs with her mother and father.

As Shelly obeyed, Paige looked directly at me and said, "I know you are here, and I know that you are watching over Shelly."

"Yes. Yes, I am. But how do you know?" I asked.

"I can hear you, and I can feel you, but I cannot see you," Paige replied. Was she blind? I was standing not two feet in front of her.

"What's your name?" she asked.

"Michael. Michael Warren," I replied.

"Well, Michael, it is nice to meet you. Can you tell me what is going on here?"

I described every incident to Paige in detail. She sat on Shelly's bed and nodded.

"You told him they should have ground his balls? Nice," she said with a little giggle. "He is a negative entity, Michael; a very nasty character. We need to get rid of him. Will you help me?"

I told her I would be thrilled to help her get this nasty bastard out of these people's lives and out of my house. Paige advised me to be ready; we would make our move tomorrow night.

Paige stayed the night with Shelly in her bed. I kept watch at the foot of the bed with my eyes never leaving the closet door. If this bastard was going to show himself, I would be ready. He didn't show up that night. Paige returned to Shelly's room after breakfast and lit some sage. She said it would weaken the man to allow her to bind him and exile him to hell or wherever the Lord decides to send him. I cannot explain it, but I trusted and believed her.

Later that afternoon, Paige walked into the room and called, "Michael, are you here with me?"

"Yes, I'm here. Are we still going to get this guy out of here tonight?" Paige said we were.

"Michael, I need you to focus. Focus all of your energy. When you do, I want you to grab the man, and I want you to push him into the portal I am going to open." I asked her how.

"Michael, are you faithful?" she asked. I said I was.

"Michael, you have more strength than you know," she responded. "You will be able to grab him and push him through. You will be the eyes that I do not have."

I agreed and steeled myself to do battle with a ghost, a ghost determined to make everyone he came in contact with miserable. He hadn't done anything to me personally except insult me, but the torture he put this little girl through, and the murder of Jack, was enough for me. I was ready.

Chapter 9

War!

Night fell, and the house was still. Paige had Shelly go downstairs with her parents. She gave Shelly's parents a golden cross and a bottle of holy water, she said some blessings and told them not to fear. Paige returned to Shelly's room and called to me. "I'm here," I responded. Paige repeated that my faith will be my strength and that I was the key to success this night. We began with a prayer that Paige said aloud to protect us. She then lit some more sage and moved about the room.

She had holy water, sea salt, and sage and a whole bag of tricks that she carried with her. I was just going to ask Paige if she thought the man had left when the closet door flew open and out he came. As I inspected him a little more closely, I could still see the bullet hole between his eyes; or rather between the two empty, black holes where his eyes should have been. I waited for the signal from Paige. She was finishing a prayer as he moved between us. He didn't speak as he moved silently toward Paige.

"Now, Michael!" Paige screamed. Grabbing to cover the man's face, I shoved him back into the closet. I pushed harder than I have ever pushed before.

"Michael, get out of there now," Paige yelled. I stumbled backward as I saw something surround the man, and then he was gone. The house actually felt lighter. "He's gone," Paige said, simply. "How about you, Michael? When are YOU going to cross?"

Chapter 10

When Will I Go Home?

I walked over to Paige and looked her in the eyes. She was staring into space. "What did you just ask me?" I said.

"I asked you, when are you going to cross over?"

"What do you mean?" I asked, my confusion growing.

Paige continued asking questions. When was the last time I had a real conversation with another person? When was the last time I left the house? When was the last time I ate? I couldn't answer her because I honestly couldn't remember. The days and nights seemed to run together, and it seemed like months passed in the blink of an eye.

Paige explained that she had looked up the history of the occupants of this house. She said that Michael Warren had died of a drug overdose from prescription medications years ago. I was in awe; I told her there must be some mistake. I didn't kill myself. She said she knew I didn't do it intentionally. Still, I didn't survive the overdose, dying on the way to the hospital. My God! No wonder my wife wouldn't speak to me. It all started to make sense.

I asked her many questions. She said my wife was fine, although she never remarried. She told me Jack died in the hospital. The man followed him there, not leaving him until Jack finished what he had started.

"Michael, it is time to go. Time for you to move on and find peace," Paige said softly.

"I can't move on! What if the man returns? What if he attacks Shelly again?"

"Michael, your battle is over. You have fulfilled your duty. The Lord wants you to come home, but the decision is yours." Paige advised me that I would not see her again unless the Lord willed it, and she hoped I would consider what we had talked about. Paige asked me to join her in saying the Lord's Prayer, and she was gone.

When she moved into the house, Shelly was a 5-year-old girl. I remained by her side in the house until, one day, I heard, "It's time to go. You don't want to be late for your own wedding, Shelly!" I stayed at her side, ever vigilant, a spiritual sentinel until it was another man's duty to stand by her.

The next few years were empty. Seasons came and went in the blink of an eye. I often wondered what Paige meant when she told me the decision to cross would be mine. With Shelly gone, I had no reason to stay. So why was I? I prayed, "Lord Jesus, bring me home to heaven." I looked around and found nothing more than the same walls.

A few years later, Shelly's parents left my house. The house became silent and still and fell into disrepair. Kids would come into the house. I would watch them to make sure that they didn't get hurt. But, what would I do if they did get hurt? It wasn't like I could call an ambulance. One night, I was standing upstairs in the bedroom where I spent my last night among the living. I reflected on the events of that night and the events that had taken place in this house over the years. I asked aloud," Lord, why am I still here? Why have you forsaken me?" No answer came.

Months passed and, one autumn night, there came a knock at my door. Although I didn't answer it, I heard the door open and close. I then heard a voice I hadn't heard in years.

"Michael? Michael, are you here?"

I got up from the floor and walked down the stairs to find a soldier in full dress uniform.

"Michael, I was sent here for you. I was sent by the Lord to bring you home," Jack told me.

"My God! Jack! You can see me?! You can hear me?"

"Michael, I heard you the night you told the voices to leave me alone. I heard you every time you tried to confront the man. I have never forgotten you."

I hugged him. "Damn, man, it is so good to see you! I can't leave. What if the man returns? What if he returns for Shelly or Paige?"

"Michael, Paige is the one that sent me. She wanted me to let you know she loves you, and she is grateful she got the chance to meet you, to meet her daddy."

"Her daddy?" I asked incredulously.

"Jack, I have no daughter. Megan and I couldn't have kids. We tried. We wanted them, but we never had any."

"The night you died, Megan had planned a dinner date with you and was going to tell you she was pregnant. She never got the chance."

"Jack, Megan was here for years! I would have seen a baby." Jack explained to me that I saw what I wanted to see of Megan. In reality, Megan moved in with my mother a week after I died. She had Paige and lived out her life caring for our daughter, never to marry again. I felt so sorry for her. Why did she not move on?

"Jack, why you? Why were you sent for me?"

"They sent me Michael because I was the first one that you were willing to sacrifice yourself for without question. They sent me because we are kindred spirits. There are no coincidences, Michael. It's time to go."

"I have to see Paige one more time, Jack. I have to see my little girl. I can't go with you. I'm sorry."

"Michael, Paige sent me. You will see her. We have to make a stop first, and then you will see Paige," Jack said.

For the first time in decades, I left my house. I followed Jack out the door, across the lawn, and ended up in a hospital. We were standing in a room, and things were unclear, but I could hear a voice over a baby crying. I walked closer to the bed, and Paige was sitting next to it, holding the hand of her daughter—and her new granddaughter. Paige turned, looked toward me, and said, "Thank you for coming to see what you created, Daddy."

"I love you. I am sorry." I hadn't seen Paige in years; my God, years!

"Daddy, it is time to go with Jack. It is time for you to go be with Mom and Grandma. I will be with you again, I promise."

Jack took me by the hand and said, "It's time, Michael." At that, I heard a voice behind me, it was Megan. She waited in the light to meet Jack and me. It had finally come for me.

PART IV

The Truth Shall Set You Free

DAN NORVELL

Chapter 1

The Truth Shall Set You Free

It was a Friday night, and I was working at the firehouse. I called home and spoke with my wife, telling her I would see her in the morning. I never made it back. The shift was uneventful; we didn't turn a wheel. On the way home, I was crossing the river and on the other side of the bridge was a car accident. I stopped to help, but it was a setup. As I looked into the car for victims, a man walked out from behind a building with a gun.

"What's going on? Where are the people from this car?" I asked.

The man simply grinned at me, "There aren't any." He lifted his gun, and in an instant, my life was over. He didn't even rob me. He just turned and walked away. I stood there, staring at my body lying in the street in a pool of blood. The man had taken most of my face off with the gun. I sat down and thought of Mary. What would happen to my wife? What would happen to my family? An odd feeling came over me, and I turned around. There, on top of the bridge, was a light. It drew me, but I never went to it. My only thought was of my wife.

I ran all the way home. It seemed like minutes, but apparently, it had been hours. By the time I made it home, there were guys from the department in and out of my house, bringing food, and their wives sat with Mary, comforting her while she cried. I had never felt so bad for anyone in my life. My funeral was huge. They carried my casket on top of the fire engine on which I served. All of the people that I worked with, in full dress uniform, walked next to the waxed and sparkling engine. The priest that delivered the sermon at my funeral gave me no comfort. I was murdered in cold blood, and there was no reason for it. I am no detective; I am a fireman.

The only thing that gunman took from me was my life. I stood in the cemetery with all of the people that I held dear. I watched as the chief presented my wife with the flag that had been draped over my casket. They lowered my casket into the ground, and everyone walked away. I stood alone, in that cemetery, with no answers, only questions. I was surprised to see a beautiful woman walk up to me and say, "Alan, it is time to go."

"Who are you?" I asked. The woman just smiled.

"I was sent here to bring you home."

"You are an angel, aren't you?" The woman nodded and looked at me sadly.

"You aren't coming with me, are you, Alan?"

"I can't. I can't leave my wife. I would rather sit here and keep an eye on her."

"Alan, all is not what it seems. The person you are now is being asked to come home. You are a good soul, and you need to come with me. If you stay, no good will come of it."

"I'm sorry. I am staying with my wife."

Looking back on that day, I wish I had followed the angel. I would come to find out that Hell was sometimes right here on earth.

Chapter 2

Stranger Than Fiction

I went home after the meeting with the angel. Mary was sitting on the couch, and I had a very funny feeling. She didn't seem the least bit upset anymore. Everyone had gone, there was just her, and she just sat there watching TV. The phone rang, and Mary said to the voice on the other end, "I can meet you tonight. I'll see you soon." I guess I was happy to see that she was not dwelling on it, but I hadn't even been in the ground for a day yet. As Mary went to get ready, there was a knock on the door. It was Joe. Mary answered the door, and her entire demeanor changed in an instant. She burst into tears and hugged Joe.

"I just miss him so much, Joe. I can't bear the thought of living without him." Joe was visibly choked up.

"That kid was like my little brother, and I feel a huge void every time I pass his locker. If you ever need anything, Mary, just call."

And with that, Joe was gone. Mary closed the door, her demeanor changing again in an instant. "Jackass," she said. I was confused. What in the hell was going on with my wife? Had she snapped? Was my death too much for her to handle? I sat on the couch as Mary moved around the house, getting ready for her meeting with the voice on the other end of the phone. I decided that I would follow her to learn more. Mary went out, started her car, and I jumped into the back seat before she left. She drove for about an hour, and it was as if she was making sure she wasn't followed. She arrived at a building in the bad part of town. She got out of the car, and I followed. She walked up some stairs and into the building.

It was a rundown apartment building, and I could hear music playing, and kids were talking behind the many doors we passed. Mary came to a door at the end of a hallway, it was room number 223. She knocked, and the door opened. A complete feeling of dread came over me. The man that opened the door was the man that had ended my life. The door closed and Mary ran to the man and kissed him.

"How long do we have to keep up the act?" the man asked.

"Just keep your cool. As soon as the insurance pays me, I'll sell the house, his truck, and everything he ever had. It will be as if he never existed."

I couldn't believe what I was witnessing. What in the hell was going on? He and Mary went into the bedroom. A few minutes later, I could hear her moaning. Clearly, I was the last thing on her mind.

I stumbled out of that apartment and all the way back to the cemetery. I stood by my grave; it hadn't even been covered for 12 hours yet. A feeling of rage came over me as I thought about it. I couldn't believe my wife had me killed! I fell onto the dirt that covered my casket. Why? Why Lord? I loved that girl with everything that I was. I felt like such a fool. Mary never gave any indication that she no longer loved me. I couldn't believe my entire marriage was for insurance money. I would never receive justice. I figured I was just a victim of a crime that would go unsolved.

I stood over my grave for hours. Days and nights ran together, and I just stood there. I never worried about anything but her for our entire marriage. Hatred and darkness filled me, I wanted justice. I heard someone walking up behind me. It was Joe. He had a bottle in his hand, and he had clearly been drinking.

"I am so sorry, Al," he sobbed. "I should have taken you to breakfast that morning. Never worry, little brother. I will always make sure Mary is taken care of." If only Joe had known.

I wish I could have told him, "Joe, you are a good man. Stay away from that bitch." I wished he could hear me. Joe stumbled away, blinded by his tears, and I felt worse than ever.

I sat propped against a tree in the cemetery for days. I was looking out across the grounds, and I noticed a man walking over toward me. He walked directly to me and said, "Hello, Al. Not having a very good afterlife, are you?"

"Who are you?"

"I am the answer to your prayers, Al. I am here to see that you receive justice."

I wasn't sure what to think. I was not quick to want to trust anyone.

"Are you an angel? Who sent you here?"

"I am an angel, of sorts. I am thinking that I can maybe help you find peace," he responded. I wanted peace now more than ever, but I was not going to agree to anything.

"Nothing is free, angel. What is the price of my justice?"

"The price is not high, just your service to me after you get your justice."

"Service to you? The only being that would ask that of me is most likely not one that I would care to take up arms with. I am standing in the presence of the devil, aren't I?"

"You are," he answered with a sly smile.

"So, if I promise to serve you for my justice, I spend eternity in hell?" I asked.

"Where are you now, Al? What kind of God would condemn you to the hell you suffer now?"

"I don't blame my misfortune on God. I blame it on Mary."

"Was Mary not created by the creator? Is she not a product of Him?"

"She is most likely a product of hell and manipulated by you. I don't believe people are created to be evil; I think they are convinced to be."

"You may be right, Al, but you may be wrong. I will leave you to your morality. But before I do, I will say this. A graveside vigil is not peace, either. If that's the way you wish to spend eternity while the man that killed you spends your blood money and screws your wife, then so be it. Good luck, Al. Have a nice afterlife."

As much as I hated to admit it, his words made sense. "What do I call you?" I asked.

"You can call me Mr. Black. It sometimes makes it easier for the ones that I work with to refer to me that way," he responded.

"I never agreed to work with you; I just asked your name."

"No need to get upset, Al. You may call me Mr. Black. You continue on your quest for eternity. I hope that God sends someone for you soon. But let me ask you this. Why should a man that risked his own life for strangers have died the way you did and not receive any justice for it? Think about that, Al. Think about it when winter gets here. Ghosts feel the cold, too. Death is not a release from misery."

"If I work for you, what would I have to do?"

"I knew you'd come around," he said. "It is really, very simple, Al. You will be given your chance for justice, and then you have to perform a task for me. After the task is performed, you will be released from anything binding. If the Lord then wants you, he can have you."

I had seen enough to realize that I couldn't let Mary and her murdering boyfriend get away with it. I wanted revenge. It made it easier to shake Mr. Black's hand.

"I'll do it, but only under one condition. Mary knows it's me taking revenge for her deeds."

"Consider it my gift to you, Al. The deal is done. You will be seen by all as a mortal, but you are not. You cannot be killed, but you can feel pain. You cannot go into any church, or walk on hallowed ground, because it will destroy you. You will have certain gifts that nobody else has. You will have the ability to disappear and return here any time you feel threatened, or you have to leave a place or situation," Black said. "After your revenge is carried out, I will advise you of the task I ask of you."

Mr. Black released my hand, and the smell of the fall air filled my nose and lungs. I was alive again, in a human body.

"Don't get too accustomed to it, Al. It is temporary. Once you are finished, the body I have granted to you will die. After that happens, I will return, and you will be sent on your task for me."

"How long do I have?"

"You take all of the time you need, Al. I have eternity for you to pay me back. Now go. Cemeteries are not a place for those such as you. The ground will begin to burn you if you stay too long. If you need to return here, do not remain long. It will kill the body that you now have."

I hurried out of the cemetery. Mr. Black wasn't kidding; the ground was starting to burn my feet. I walked to the nearest gas station and asked to use their restroom. I entered and looked into the mirror. Mr. Black had granted me a body that looked like a bodybuilder. I was perfect. I felt the hatred for Mary run through the blood in my veins. I would begin to figure out what I was going to do to get my revenge against her and the man that killed me.

DAN NORVELL

Chapter 3

Twisted Fate

The need for vengeance filled my heart. My beating heart! I was once again alive! It was a wonderful feeling to breathe air into my lungs again. I would be able to eat, to feel. I started toward home. I felt empty, but I was OK with it. I was alive! As I walked, I came closer and closer to a church. The closer I got, the weaker I felt. I had to cross the street and hurry by. Mr. Black wasn't kidding. It caused me to become weak and actually felt painful. I wouldn't make that mistake twice.

As I walked home, I passed a house where I could hear a little girl screaming. "Stop, Daddy! Stop!" I had a strange awareness; I could hear and feel the little girl's pain and anguish. I stopped and walked up to the door. I knocked but nobody answered. I could hear the little girl screaming louder. I dropped back, and I kicked the door in. I ran up the stairs and there, on the floor of a bathroom, was a man attacking his daughter. She couldn't have been more than 8 years old. I grabbed the man by the shoulder and threw him across the room without effort, he hit the wall in the hallway and got right back up. I turned and glared at him.

"You sick prick. What in the hell is wrong with you? How could you hurt your own little girl, your baby?!?"

"Who the hell are you? What gives you the right to bust into my house?"

"That little girl's screams gave me that right, and, now, you are going to pay!"

The man hit me in the mouth, but I barely felt it. I grabbed him by the throat and tossed him down the hall and against a door. He grabbed the handle and hurried through the door. As I made it to the room, the man had a gun pointed at me. I put my hands up.

"Calm down. You don't need your daughter to see this. I'll just leave."

The man began squeezing the trigger. The bullets passed through me, and they burned. I looked down and saw no blood. There were bullet holes in the wall behind me.

I looked the man in the face. "You can't kill a dead man."

"What are you?" he asked, his eyes wide with terror.

"I am the strength and revenge that your daughter does not have. I am your worst nightmare!" A couple of more shots were fired, and I heard a groan behind me. I turned in time to see the little girl crumple to the floor. The bullets had passed through me and into her.

"My God! What have I done?" the man screamed.

I knew she was dead the instant her little body hit the floor. I turned and looked back at the man. We could hear sirens. A neighbor must have called the police when the man shot at me the first time. I had to get out of here. As I started to run, I was immediately back in the cemetery. Mr. Black was standing there, at my graveside, looking at me.

"You weren't kidding. I just thought of getting out of there, and I was here!" Mr. Black backhanded me, and my body hit the tree behind my grave.

"I did not grant you this gift to be an avenging angel. You take care of your business, and that is it. I am not making deals to make you feel better."

"That little girl deserved to be protected. I tried to help her."

"It is not your concern to protect the innocent anymore. You did a bang-up job, Al. She's dead. I had plans for her father, and now he may repent for the sins he committed. You have probably cost me a soul. It had better not happen again, or I'll return you to this grave, bind your soul inside of that shell that used to be you, and you can spend eternity in the cold ground. Are we clear?"

"We are," I responded, silently grieving for the little girl I was unable to save.

"Now get out of here. You make me sick."

With that, he was gone, and the burning began in my feet. I hurried out of the cemetery once again. What a twisted fate. I am a good man, or at least I was. I feel alive, but not really. Those bullets passed through me like I wasn't even there. Flesh would have slowed them at the very least. I can't believe I could have been so stupid. I cost that innocent girl her life. The day I died, I should have just followed the angel. I could have been in the company of the Lord now, and maybe I would not feel the need for revenge. Now all I have is a debt to pay to the devil and no chance for peace. Ever.

Chapter 4

The Cost of Revenge

I knew what Mr. Black said to me was not just a threat, it was a promise. I knew my fate would be worse if I crossed him again. I decided I would take my revenge and complete my end of the bargain. After that, I would perform the task he asks and wander the earth if that would be my fate. I decided to head for the apartment where my wife went after my funeral. I decided to repay the man that killed me. I wondered how I would take my revenge on him. I thought that maybe I would strangle him, or perhaps I would throw him out his window into the street. This man had taken everything from me. He had helped Mary trick me and made me feel something real. All I could think of was killing him. I was not sure what I was, but I knew I would have the first half of my revenge very soon.

I finally made it to the apartment, but the man wasn't there. I broke the door handle and went inside. I wanted him to come in and fight, he would not be able to hurt me anyway. It would be better for me if he did fight. Then I would not feel so much remorse when I took his life. I sat on the man's couch and waited for him to return. It was about three hours later when he returned home.

"Evenin', Sunshine," I said.

"Who the hell are you?"

"I am vengeance," I responded, grabbing him by the throat and lifting him at least a foot off the floor. I was amazed at my own strength. The man's eyes grew wild as I choked off his air supply. He gripped my arm with both of his hands, but his efforts were useless. The body that Mr. Black had granted me was far too strong.

As the man's eyes began to roll back into his head, I remembered that I had sworn to protect the lives and property of this city, even his. I released my grip and dropped him to the floor.

"I am a friend of the man you killed, and I'm here to kill you," I said.

The man, holding his throat, spoke. "It was her idea. I didn't want to kill anybody."

"I don't believe you," I replied.

The man got up from the floor and ran into the kitchen; I followed. I was met in the kitchen by the man pointing the same gun that killed me at my face.

"Now, you can find out how your friend died." The man opened fire, and the bullets passed through me without any damage. I walked up to him and grabbed the gun. He was still squeezing the trigger, and I felt his arm break as I snatched the gun from him. He screamed in pain and, before I realized what I was doing, I snapped his neck like a toothpick. His lifeless body slumped to the floor. I turned to find Mr. Black standing behind me.

"Excellent, Al. I wasn't sure if the revenge you felt in your heart would allow you to commit murder. I am pleased to be wrong."

"You aren't wrong. I simply reacted to being shot. Before I was aware, I snapped his neck."

"I don't care how it happened, Al. It happened. One down and one to go."

"What about him?" I asked, nodding toward the dead man.

"I will be escorting his dark soul to hell momentarily, Al. You have the rest of the job to finish, so go and finish it."

I watched as Mr. Black reached into the man's body and pulled out his soul by his hair. The man looked at me in terror. He and Mr. Black disappeared into a shadow. I wondered if that would be the way I would be taken to hell after I finished my task for Mr.

Black. I heard the sound of voices heading toward the apartment. I ducked into the bathroom as police burst in. I thought of returning to the cemetery, and I was there in an instant. Night was falling as I hurried out of the cemetery, I needed to go to my house. It was time to repay Mary for her sin.

DAN NORVELL

Chapter 5

Mary's Payment

As I walked toward my house, I was conflicted with feelings of revenge and remorse. I was genuinely sorry that I had taken the man's life. I simply reacted to him shooting at me; it was not intentional. I dropped him, and I think I would have left, but he came at me shooting so I acted out of instinct. I stopped a few blocks from my house. Was it my destiny to kill Mary?

"Now, you are thinking, Al." I turned to see a young girl standing behind me.

"Who are you?" I asked.

"I am one possibility if you do not continue on the course you have set. I am yours and Mary's unborn child."

"What? Mary wasn't pregnant," I told the girl.

"Yes, she is, and even though she is a bad person, maybe the life she brings into the world will change her. Al, it is not your decision to be the judge of Mary. It is God's."

"I have made a deal with the devil. I have to hold up my end of the bargain."

"It is not just Mary that you will kill, Al. The death of the man was self-defense; this will be cold-blooded murder. You are a protector, not a murderer. Do you really think that the devil intends to make good on his end of the deal? He is a liar."

"What will happen to you without a father?"

"You are part of me. I will be strong. My mother will never speak of you, but Joe will. I will know you because of your friend. I want to know who you were by your goodness, not think that you are in peril because of the hell you suffered for revenge."

The girl was gone. I looked around in confusion. I had no place to go, so I walked to a park and sat in one of the swings. I couldn't kill my own daughter. Nobody knew Mary had me killed but me. I was just getting up from the swing when I was faced with a man in a white suit, bathed in a brilliant white light.

"Al, you have been deceived. You are not the man that Mr. Black has made you think you are."

"Who are you?" I asked.

"I am another angel sent for you. I am an angel strong enough to combat Mr. Black if he decides to show his cowardly face."

"What have I become? What am I?"

"You are a product of Mr. Black's quest for your soul. He is trying to prove to God that even the good souls like yours are not off-limits to him."

I could not believe I had been so stupid. "What of Mary and my daughter?" I asked.

"Your love for your wife was real. Mary is mentally unstable, and your friend Joe will be the protector of your daughter. He and his wife will raise her as their own. Joe loved you, Al. Do not taint all that you were by becoming what Mr. Black wants you to be."

"How do I get out of the deal I made with Mr. Black?"

"You have not yet committed a sin in the Lord's eyes. The death of the man that killed you, you have shown remorse for, and he forgives you. Do not make the same mistake twice. You will not be forgiven again."

I felt sick. I was losing my strength. "What is happening?" I asked the angel.

"The body is dying, Al. You need to get to the church and get inside. It will kill the body and release your soul on sacred ground. I will be there to take you home." I started to walk toward the church, weakening with every step. I looked up, and I was on the steps of the church. I heard a voice behind me.

"I will have a soul, Al. I will take the soul of your daughter!" The angel was standing in the door of the church, his hand outstretched.

"Come on, Al. He is a liar. This is the only way you will be able to protect her from him."

I reached up and grasped the angel's hand, and everything went black. I stood and looked down at the melting remains of the body that I had occupied. It became water, forming a puddle on the church steps.

"You resisted Mr. Black, Al. He will not be able to bother you anymore," the angel told me.

"What about my daughter? What will happen to her? I have made a dangerous enemy in Mr. Black."

"Your daughter will be fine," the angel assured me.

"The only parents she will ever know will be Joe and his wife. Mary will be gone before your daughter is 6 months old."

"What will happen to Mary?" I asked the angel.

"Mary will end up where she belongs. She was only the vessel for your daughter, Al. She will not be around to leave any lasting impression. You daughter is the miracle of your life. She will end up being a doctor, and she will be happy. Out of the pain that you suffered and Mary's sins, your daughter will be the good that came of it."

"What is Hell, angel? Where is it?"

"Al, you were already there. I rescued your good soul from hell."

There was a bright light, and I knew, then and there, that the truth had truly set me free.

PART V

Faith No More

DAN NORVELL

Chapter 1

Faith No More

How was I going to find this kid when I have been dead for more than 50 years? The world has changed so much in that time. I have observed the senseless acts of many in the time since I took my last breath on this Earth. I have just seven short days, to find a boy and make him aware that he is more than what he realizes. The world is such an unfriendly place. I cannot think of a worse time to need humanity to be faithful. I was given seven days, and only five were left. I'm not sure where I am. I know I am in the Midwest United States. Not much else is clear to me. The boy resides in this city, and I have to find him. I cannot fail. If I fail, humanity ends. If humanity ends, it means that it was a mistake.

I remember the Archangel Michael said to me, "Father, you have been chosen. You have been chosen for your faith. If humanity is proven to be a mistake, Heaven and Earth will crumble. Never forget what is at stake, Father. Never forget that eternity hangs on the soul of this one boy." A lot was riding on my shoulders. I have never lost faith, but my faith has always been in the Lord. Now, I need to have faith in myself. I often think that maybe Michael should have picked another candidate.

I was sitting in a Catholic church, praying that I can find this boy. It was around midday, and the church had only two other people in it. They were near the front of the church, praying. The door in the back opened and closed. A boy walked in and lay down on the pew next to me. He looked tired. He looked like he hasn't eaten in days. The door opened once more, the boy curled up tight and there he stayed, very still. Two boys walked in, one with a gun in hand. They looked around and left.

The boy, still lying there, asked, "Are they gone, Father?"

"They are," I replied.

"What is your name, son?"

"My name is Peter. I don't know my last name, Father. I never had one. They don't assign last names at the orphanage."

"Why were those boys chasing you, Peter?" I asked.

"They were going to kill a puppy in the alley over on Jackson Street. I shoved the one with the gun, and the puppy ran. They chased me and shot once. I know the bullet came close. I could hear it whiz by my ear."

I placed my hand on Peter's arm and said, "Son, you rest. I will be sitting right here when you wake."

The exhausted boy fell asleep within minutes. I knew I had found the boy I sought.

Chapter 2

The Story of Good vs. Evil

Peter slept for hours. As promised, I didn't leave his side. He finally stirred and asked, "Father, why do bad things have to happen?"

"Son, bad things happen to everyone, every day. The Lord never gives you more than you can deal with. Always keep in mind, Peter, that if everything in the world was good all of the time, many people would have nothing to look forward to and no reason for faith. The bad is sometimes what makes us cherish those good times even more."

Peter smiled, "I guess you're right, Father."

He proceeded to tell me that he only had blurred visions of his parents. He could not remember the last time he had seen them and that, one day, they were just gone. The orphanage was not a friendly place. He lifted his shirt to show me the scars across his back.

"Father, do you think that losing my parents could have been wrong? Do you think that maybe it should have happened to someone else instead of me?"

"Let me tell you a story, son. It is a story that has been told many times in many ways. This is my gift to you because I have never shared it with anyone."

I told Peter of a time when Heaven and Earth were closer than they are now. I told him of an angel so beautiful and wise that the Lord cherished him. The Lord has no favorites, but the Lord really felt that this angel was more than the rest. It made the Lord proud, but it also made Him uneasy at the same time. Pride can be a source of good, but it can also prove to be very bad.

The Lord created man. Mankind cherished the Lord, and the Lord loved them. Over time, humanity began to show the pride that the angel did. The angel had been coming to Earth and placing false ideas into the mind of mankind. The Lord called on the angel and asked him why. The angel replied that he could be a better creator than the Lord. The Lord cast him out of Heaven and gave him his own realm to rule and create in. That realm is Hell. Before his departure, the angel told the Lord that mankind was a mistake. If the angel were ever to prove this, Heaven and Earth would collide and crumble; all existence as we know it would no longer be. The Lord had a safeguard in place—he could wipe out humanity, such as he did with a great flood, and cleanse the Earth of mankind. If mankind no longer exists, there is no mistake. The angel, so twisted by his own pride and envy of our Lord, promised that he would never stop trying to make the Lord realize his mistake. It is better for the angel, who is now the creator of the realm of demons, to bide his time and let his twisted beliefs bleed through into our world and ultimately try to prove that the Lord is wrong. If that ever were to happen, we would all be wiped from the slate of creation.

Peter stared at me in awe. He finally spoke. "Father? Do you think it is possible? Do you think that the angel will be able to prove that mankind was a mistake?"

"Son, every day Mothers kill their babies, children are killing children. Sin is all about us, everywhere," I replied. "It is being committed without repenting. I think, Peter, that if mankind were ever to be proven to be a mistake... here and now would be the chance that the angel needs. Mankind has one chance. It can be saved by one soul. That soul has to realize that he is more than what he appears. His worth may not appear to be much here, but the very fabric of existence hangs on him. I only hope that he realizes it in time."

Peter shuddered. "I hope he does, Father. I hope he does." Peter laid back down; the poor boy hadn't slept in days. "Father, do you care if I sleep some more here? It's the only place I feel safe; the only place that is calm."

"Rest for the night, child. I will remain at your side for as long as you need me to," I responded. Peter fell asleep with a smile on his face. I placed my hand on his head and prayed. I prayed this boy would realize that he was the key to existence. The fate of humanity, the fate of creation, rested on his shoulders. As Peter slept, one day melted into the next, one day closer to the end.

DAN NORVELL

Chapter 3

Answers Lead to More Questions

Peter slept for the rest of the night and most of the morning. He finally woke up and told me he was hungry. I hadn't felt hunger in many years, so I told Peter to walk over to the basket by the door and take out enough money for breakfast. It was my feeling that it was more important for the church to feed this hungry boy than anything else those few dollars might be used for. We walked a few blocks to a small diner and sat in a booth. I could smell the coffee; I missed the taste of coffee. Peter placed his order and asked if I would like some coffee. The waitress stared at Peter as if he were crazy. I raised my hand and shook my head no.

As Peter ate, he described to me the final days he had spent with his parents and little sister. He said that he missed all of them very much and was unclear about the events that had taken them from him. Peter told me that he was riding his new bicycle that his parents had just given him for his birthday and that he was riding very fast. He was not sure how, but he was thrown from the bike, hit his head, and was knocked out. When he awoke, Peter's bike was nowhere to be found, so he walked home. When he arrived home, his parents and sister were gone. I found his story very odd, but I did not question him about it. I had seen his scars; someone had taken him to that orphanage, and Peter may have blocked it from his mind. He paid the waitress, and we left the diner. We spent the day walking and talking, and I was not sure when we were going to be made aware of any event on the horizon. We walked by a park, and Peter stopped in his tracks.

"What's wrong, son?" I asked.

"That's the park where the voices are, Father. The voices call to me every time I pass this park; they call to me to come into the light. The light took my parents and my little sister. I stay away because I don't want it to take me, too." The boy's voice trembled. Clearly, he was terrified of this park or whatever was in it that created the chatter that Peter was hearing.

"I think they are ghosts, Father." This was a difficult situation for me to discuss with Peter since I'm a ghost. To this boy, I was as real as he is.

"Son, they may or may not be ghosts but have faith that the Lord will not let them harm you. Your faith will see you through the darkest of times."

We walked for a few more hours, and I found something very odd. The city was very loud but, as we walked, we didn't pass anyone. I had not seen a single car drive by, yet I could hear traffic all around. Dusk was coming, and Peter asked if we could return to the church because he said he felt cold. We made our way back to the church, and I could swear that the church was on the opposite corner of the intersection than when we left this morning. We entered the church. The benches were a different color, and the candles were in different places. Something is very wrong here, I thought to myself. The same two people, a man, and a woman still prayed. They faced toward the alter and paid no attention to Peter. In all my years as a priest, this was the first time I had ever felt uneasy in a church. Something was not right, and I now lost another day looking for the answers I needed to help this boy save humanity.

Chapter 4

The Trip to the Park

Peter slept restlessly that night. I knew we needed to return to the park for answers. Peter jerked awake.

"Father! Father!"

"Yes? I am here, son." Peter appeared very upset and confused.

"Father, I can hear my sister and parents calling my name. They were calling to me all night long like I was dreaming it."

I told the boy that I was not sure what it could mean, but I assured him that I would stay with him as long as I could. I asked Peter if he was hungry and he said he wasn't. He told me that, even when he eats, his stomach still feels empty. There were so many things going on that I could not explain, and this was another one. I had watched that boy eat like a horse, and now it made sense why he ate so much. I was running out of time; I needed to get to that park. It was the park that held the key. It's where the battle will begin. Peter and I needed to go there to stop whatever was coming.

I spent the next three hours trying to convince Peter to return to the park with me. He finally agreed under one condition: I had to promise I would stay by his side and not leave him.

"Son, I will not leave your side if I don't have to. Know this here and now—you are by far one of the bravest boys I have ever met, and someday you will change the world. That much I can assure you."

We set out for the park. The day was hot, and there was a strange odor in the air. It smelled of a hospital. I recognized the smell from all of the times I had visited hospitals to administer the Last Rights to the dead and dying. Peter and I walked in silence. I had more questions than answers. What is this boy to do? Has he not suffered enough? What could be in this park to bring about the end of all creation? We arrived at the park, and I found it odd that it seemed farther from the church than it did yesterday. Peter was clearly apprehensive.

"Don't you hear them, Father? Don't you hear the voices calling to me? They are calling my name!" I heard nothing but the wind gently rustling the trees.

"What are the voices saying, son?"

"They are asking me to come into the light, to come home." I wasn't sure what it all meant, but we continued on into the park. Peter seemed even more melancholy.

"Father, the voices want me to come into the light, but all I can see is a darkened park!"

Maybe something will come to us."

We walked for what seemed to be hours, and, suddenly, we were at the front gates of the park where we had entered.

"Peter, we have walked in a straight line ever since we entered this park, have we not?"

"Yes, Father, we have. Why are we back at the front gates?" I didn't have an answer for him.

"Let's return to the church, Peter. The night is coming, and I am not sure we should be out in it when it arrives."

Peter clutched my sleeve. "Father, we won't have very far to go."

The church was now across the street from the park. I just stood there, awestruck. There was not a church there before, let alone the very church where we spent the last two nights.

"What does it mean, Father?"

"I don't know, son, but whatever it means, we need to get inside."

There were two reasons we needed to get into the church. The first was that night was coming. The second was that I could hear the voices calling to the boy.

DAN NORVELL

Chapter 6

Peter's Gift

It was fall, although I don't know the year. For the second time since my death, I am being sent to help the same boy. St. Michael told me I was going to witness an event, and Peter would need me.

"It's time for you to go back, Father."

"I am ready."

The next thing I knew, I was standing in a house watching a man shave. He looked into the mirror, and I looked at the reflection. Those eyes gave him away in an instant: it was Peter. He put on his shirt, slung his gun holster over his shoulder, and then put on his coat. Peter had become a police officer. I followed him into the living room.

"Hello, son," I said, but he couldn't hear or see me. I thought it best that I follow Peter and see if I could figure out what I needed to do for him.

Peter worked for the Secret Service in the nation's capital. He was assigned to the high priority division that protects diplomatic visitors to America. I heard Peter's superior tell him he was to protect the Pope tonight at a speech. This Pope had been instrumental in trying to negotiate peace in some pretty nasty spots in the world, and many people would like to see him harmed. Peter spent most of his day doing paperwork and studying the set up for his assignment. He would be the agent closest to the Pope. The other guys teased him on the way out of the office that day.

"See you in the pressure cooker tonight, Pete."

"See you tonight, guys," he responded with a smile.

Peter went home to gather his things and relax. Before he left, he got a phone call from his mother. "Say hello to the Pope for me and be careful, son."

"I always am, Mom. Goodnight."

Peter went to his closet and pulled out a small box. He removed a small crucifix from the box and placed it around his neck. Last, he put on his bulletproof vest and his gun.

"Father, if you are still with me; if you are still watching, please watch over my team tonight."

"I will, son." I could tell that Peter was apprehensive about his assignment. He was very nervous about something. Anytime you have a Pope visit, it has to be a dangerous event for all involved. It was time to start the banquet. The team was briefing, and Peter's superior said, "Pete, I am sticking you on point. I need my best man closest to the Pope." Peter nodded.

The Pope arrived and started to speak. The crowd was enormous. As the Pope spoke, a man stood up and reached into his jacket. Peter started to reach into his jacket as well, but the man pulled out a napkin to blow his nose. I could see Peter shake his head and continue to scan the crowd. Dinner was being served, and waiters moved among the tables. The Holy Father continued his speech, and the crowd listened while they ate. I remembered the first time I had seen a Pope speak years ago. I knelt and said a prayer for this Pope and for the people there. I asked the Lord to look out for Peter and his team tonight. As I finished praying, the wait staff started to serve desert. I thought to myself, a little bit longer, and Peter is finished with his assignment. Maybe Michael sent me here to watch over Peter.

The waiter picking up trays at the table directly in front of the Pope spun around. "Gun!" is all I heard before two shots rang out. After the second shot was fired, I saw the waiter slump to the ground. There was a lot of commotion, and the Holy Father was rushed from the building in about 10 seconds flat. I made my way to the front of the room. What I saw made me sick. Peter lay on the floor in front of where the Pope had been speaking. He was shot in the throat, and one of the officers with him was holding pressure on it.

"Stay with me, Pete. Stay with me!" I could see Peter drifting in and out of consciousness, and his blue eyes fixed on me. He tried to speak, but nothing came out. I knelt beside him as his eyes were fixed on mine. He tried to say, "Father..."

"Peter, I am here, son. I am here to bring you home." Peter gasped, and his eyes began to roll back into his head. The paramedics arrived, loaded Peter into the ambulance, and raced to the hospital. The doctors worked for two hours to try to save Peter. I waited. I was sitting outside Peter's room when a boy walked up to me and said, "Father? Is there someone here for you to see?"

I asked the boy, who I had never seen before, "Son, you can see me?"

"Of course, Father. All of us here can see you." I looked up, and I was no longer in the hospital. I was standing in a room filled with children.

"Where am I?" I asked.

"You were about to say the opening prayer for our breakfast, Father. Are you OK?"

Was I dreaming? I was back in my church, and it was the morning of my death. I wondered why Michael was letting me see this. I shook my head and turned around to lead the prayer, but the church was empty. I was standing in a funeral home, and a priest was talking with Peter's parents, his sister, and her children. I moved closer to the conversation.

"I was just a boy when Father O'Brien died," the priest said. "I was the last one to speak with him that morning. I asked him if he was OK, and he had a stroke. He died before he hit the ground. I remember his gentle face and his reassuring eyes, but Father O'Brien was dead for years before your son was born."

Peter's mother spoke, "Peter had an accident when he was younger. While he was in a coma, he said that a priest helped him find our voices in the light. The reason I am asking is that when Peter died, he kept mouthing 'Father, Father take me with you.'"

The priest shook his head, "It defies explanation. I know if I were to have a guardian angel, Father O'Brien would be the one I'd choose."

The priest gave a sermon later at the church and called Peter a hero. He explained that not only did Peter serve his country, but he also served the Lord by saving the Holy Father. The priest then read a note written by the Pope himself, commending Peter and his bravery and extending his condolences to Peter's family. I followed the procession to the cemetery and watched as they laid Peter to rest. I stood there for a long time after the people had gone. I said a prayer and looked toward the sky.

"Michael? What am I supposed to do? This boy gave his life, and I am still not sure what the mission is."

I heard a voice behind me, "Father? Thank you for coming. I always knew you would be the one that the Lord would send for me should I ever pass in the line of duty." It was Peter.

"I wish I hadn't seen you again in this way, son. It was an honorable thing you did for the Holy Father; the reason you needed to survive when you were a boy."

"I know, Father. I have never forgotten you. I saw you there at my side after the shooting, and I saw you at the hospital. I am ready to go with you now, Father."

Peter and I set out across the cemetery and into the light of Heaven. A year later, the Pope helped the countries of the world disarm their nuclear arsenals. If Peter had not saved the Holy Father, it never would have happened. He saved humanity, and he had faith to know that God would send me for him when he took that bullet. Heaven and Earth would not crumble because this boy proved that it is not a mistake. There were still people in the world that held faith in humanity. The faith of one man did save creation. The fallen angel would have to wait another few thousand years when humanity again began to forget the Lord that put them here. The actions of one person saved all of creation. The sad thing to me was that nobody on Earth will ever be aware of the true hero that Peter was. Peter did what Jesus did: he died for all of their sins.

PART VI

Funeral for a Friend

Chapter 1

Silent Treatment

I was never so pissed in my entire life. I had done everything for this girl, who did she think she was? I sped out of her driveway and squealed my tires the whole way. I was going to find my so-called best friend, and most likely kick his ass for kissing on my girlfriend. I finally got onto the main road and put the pedal down. I must have been doing 110 mph. When I hit the back end of the parked truck, I don't think I had even let off the accelerator at all. I remember a bunch of lights, and some guy telling me it was going to be alright, and then laying in a hospital bed with a bunch of people around me. I heard someone say "Clear!" and I felt electricity pierce through my body. That guy did that about five more times, and I heard him say, "That's it, call it." I heard a woman say, "Time of death, 23:34."

DEATH? What was she talking about? Who had died? I walked out into the waiting room to find my family with my best friend, and girlfriend sitting and waiting.

I walked up to Tom, "Hey buddy, I guess it's ok to kiss my girlfriend and then come see me at the hospital." Tom just stared blankly into my face.

A doctor came out and asked to speak with my parents, "I bet they think I was drinking. It is two weeks from graduation, I am not drinking anything until after that. Tom. TOM! Answer me, damn you!"

I heard my mother scream, and my father was holding her in his arms. The doctor walked away, saying, "I am sorry." What was he sorry about? I was going to be in deep shit when Dad finds out the new car they just bought is wrecked. My parents walked out into the waiting room where Sarah and Tom were still standing. "He didn't make it," my father told them. What are they talking about? I am standing right here. Sarah started screaming and latched onto Tom. "Great! Now you have to cheat with him in front of me?" I am getting the feeling that I am getting the silent treatment.

"What happened?" My mother had asked Sarah.

"We had a fight, and he left my house upset. He thought I was cheating on him with Tom. We were planning a surprise party for his 18th birthday, and someone saw me kiss Tom on the cheek for all of his help. I would never have done anything to hurt him, but he wouldn't believe me!"

I started to yell, "Hey! I am right here! I didn't know, Sarah. Would one of you talk to me?"

They all walked out and left me standing there in the waiting room. I thought they were all crazy, and I decided just to walk home, the hospital was only a mile from my house anyway. I began to walk home, and a man in a long dark trench coat walked up to me.

"Where are you going, kid?" I had never seen the man before in my life.

"I am heading home, who are you?"

"I'll be watching you. You'll know who I am soon enough."

I turned to tell this psycho to back off, and he was gone as quickly as he appeared. I finally got home, went to my room, and went to bed. I was tired, and I knew that once everything had sunk in, my father was going to read me the riot act in the morning.

I woke up the next morning and looked at the clock. "Holy cow! It was 10:30 in the morning!" My mother had not woken me for school. I got up and ran into my parent's bedroom. My father was still in bed, and my mother was not in the bedroom at all. I went downstairs, and my mother was sitting in a chair, staring out the window.

116

"Mom? Why didn't you wake me up? It's Friday, and I'm late!" I didn't even change and ran out of the door and all the way to school. I went straight to my algebra class and walked through the open door.

"I am sorry, Mr. Kinney, my mother, didn't wake me up." Mr. Kinney didn't say a word, and nobody even looked up. I could not figure out why everyone was acting this way. The bell rang about a half-hour later, and I went to find Tom to apologize.

I felt like a complete ass for thinking about what I had thought. The school was the quietest I had ever seen. Kids were walking through the hallways without speaking. I had a few minutes before my next class, and I went to talk with Coach. I knew that Coach would talk to me no matter what. I went and knocked on his door, and nobody answered. The coach was never out of the office at this time of day. I'll just stand here and wait for a few minutes, and I'll catch up with Tom and Sarah later and patch things up there. Coach walked out of his office, "Coach, can we talk for a minute?" He ignored me and walked right by me like I didn't even exist. I just stood there, shaking my head.

"What in the hell did I do to everyone? Did I just walk into the Twilight Zone?" I needed to find Tom and Sarah, I know they might be mad, but they would talk to me. I walked down an empty hallway, and at the end of it was the man in the trench coat.

"Bobby? Haven't you figured it out yet? Don't you know why nobody will talk to you?" I ran toward that guy full blast, by the time I got there, he was gone. I wasn't sure what was going on, but I was going to find out.

Chapter 2

The Funeral

What was going on here? Everyone was ignoring me, and this guy in the trench coat is really starting to make me mad. I was about at my wit's end. There has to be an explanation, and I intended to find it. I walked down the hallway, and everyone just seemed to ignore me. I didn't care, if they can't understand how I felt about just smashing my father's new car, then I didn't need to talk to any of them anyhow. I walked out of school and headed home; I couldn't find Tom or Sarah anywhere. When I got home, the Priest from our church was there at my house.

I walked in and said, "Hello, Father." Father ignored me as well. I must really have done something bad here. Even Father is ignoring me. "I'll be in my room if anyone cares!" Nobody answered. I was beat. I slumped into the big chair in my room and tried to turn the TV on. It wouldn't work. A perfect end to a perfect day. I just went to sleep.

I woke up to a house full of people and a bunch of boxes in my room. "Jeez, how long did I sleep?" I went downstairs, and everyone was dressed as they had just attended a funeral. "Who died?" I asked. Nobody answered.

The man in the trench coat answered me, though, "You did Bobby. You died four nights ago in a car accident."

I turned and looked at the man, "What did you just say?"

"I said you're dead, Bobby. You let emotions get the better of you, and you paid the highest price of all, with your life."

I tried to grab the man from the arm, and all I got was a handful of nothing. "Where did you go?!? Who are you? What happened?"

The man was gone. I couldn't believe him, and I wouldn't believe him. I would find the answer to prove him wrong. I walked back downstairs and up to my mother, "Mom, you and I need to talk right now." My mother ignored me. I walked out of the house and to the local cemetery. A funeral had just taken place, and I walked to the gravesite of the burial. There was not a gravestone there yet, but many people that I recognized left flowers on the grave.

Sarah came walking up the gravesite, "Goodbye, Bobby, I had always hoped we would be together longer than this."

I looked at her, "Sarah, I haven't gone anywhere. Why are you all treating me this way?"

Sarah walked out of the cemetery, and an older looking man walked up to me. "It doesn't get any easier, son. It is hard to let go, that's why I am still here after 60 years."

I looked at the man, "What?" As I stared at him, he began to back away, "It never gets any easier, son, unless you cross."

He turned and walked right into a massive gravestone and disappeared. Maybe I was dead, maybe it wasn't a dream… more like a nightmare. I had the world by the horns, a girlfriend, a bright future, a free ride through college for football, and I pissed it all away by getting mad for no reason.

I fell to my knees, "Why God? Why did you do this to me?"

I heard a voice from behind me, "God had nothing to do with it, Bobby. This one is all you."

I turned to see the man in the trench coat looking at me. "What is going on?" I asked. The man in the trench coat would finally reveal to me what was going on.

"I am Death, Bobby. Many have called me different things throughout the ages, but Death is the best description."

I asked, "Is this Heaven, or Hell?"

Death replied, "It is neither Heaven or Hell. It is where you are until you make a choice. I am neither good or evil, I just am here to do a job, and now my job is finished. It will be entirely up to you where you will spend eternity."

"Up to me? What do you mean?"

"You have a few choices, Bobby. You can cross into one of two places, Heaven or Hell, or you can stay here. It will be up to you. You will only stay as long as you want to, and you will encounter others along the way. Nobody living will hear or see you. Right now, you are a lost soul, you were taken before your time, by your own actions. God has no place for you yet, it was not your time."

"If it wasn't my time, then why did it happen?"

Death again replied, "It happened because you are ultimately in charge of your own destiny. God was not ready for you for years yet, but because of your anger, you forced me to come here before an angel could make it to your side to perform a miracle."

I asked him, "A miracle? You mean I didn't have to die?"

"Bobby, you didn't have to drive like a maniac, it was your choice. The truck that you hit sat there because someone broke down and was walking to a house to use their phone. The angel did perform a miracle that night, he chose to have you hit the truck, and sacrifice yourself rather than the van with three kids and two parents in it a mile up the road. The very same people that called the ambulance; that carried you to the hospital. I came for you because the angel made his choice based on your reckless behavior."

"I cannot have a second chance?"

"How many times have you driven like that, Bobby? How many second chances do you think you are entitled to? I have to leave, but I will tell you this much… where you will spend eternity is up to you. You will have to decide who and what you believe, and that will determine where you end up. Goodbye, Bobby."

He was gone. He left me with more questions than answers. I decided to walk home and sit with my parents for a while. Even though they couldn't see or hear me, maybe they would know I was there by me just being home.

Chapter 3

The Lady in White

I had been dead for about two months now, and I just sat and watched my mother sink into a more profound depression. I was their only child, and the void I had left was becoming overwhelming for her. I knew my mother was having issues with me leaving for college, but this was something she never expected and should have not ever had to deal with. I was so stupid, and I can remember Death saying to me, "How many second chances do you deserve?" It made me think of the many times I had driven crazy and been reckless with Sarah in the car, or if I had hit that family… maybe they would be dead as well. In the grand design, I would have made the same choice the angel had made.

I was sitting in the living room with my mother when a knock came to the door, it was Sarah. She had come by to check on my mother, and to say goodbye. She would be leaving early for college, and honestly, who would blame her?

"I would have stayed home longer if Bobby was here. I just miss him so much." My mother hugged Sarah, and said, "I miss him too, but I can feel him every day. I know he is watching us."

I couldn't stand the moment any longer and ran out of the house. I stood outside for a long time, and a lady walked into the yard where I was standing.

"Bobby, I am the angel that was to save you the night of your accident." I looked at her, she was beautiful.

"Why are you here?" I asked.

"I am here to see if you forgive me. I had a choice to make that night, and I chose life for five instead of one. It was my decision, and the consequence was that I would be cast out until I was forgiven for my choice."

I looked into her beautiful eyes, "I would have made the same choice. You are forgiven."

The angel began to weep. "I have one thing to tell you, Bobby. You will have to decide where your eternity will be. You will be tempted along the way by different things, follow your heart, and your faith... it will lead you home. I will be there waiting for you when you have made the right choices."

The angel turned and walked across the yard. A brilliant light started to shine onto her, and she was gone. I remembered what she had said, and I wondered what it meant. I stared into the sky, "I want to be the best I can be, Lord, but how can I do that now?" I walked back into my house and went to my room. I thought of all of the things that seemed important to me in life, football games, Friday night dates with Sarah, that car, and it all seemed unimportant to me now. Things seemed to be part of a much grander design, and I now needed to figure out what was really important to me, my morals and faith would be all I have left to decide what would become of me.

A month later, my mother was looking through some old photos of us with my father. She pulled a photo out, and I recognized the face instantly. The face in the picture was the face of the angel that talked with me and asked for my forgiveness. It was the face of my grandmother.

"She was twenty when this picture was taken, she had me two years later, and died when I was three."

My mother had never shown me that picture before, I wondered why the angel was my grandmother. My father asked how she died, and my mother explained that she had a terrible drinking problem and had gotten deeply depressed after she had her. She had never had the chance to really know her mom; she had gotten drunk one night and cut her wrists in the bathtub. She died before anyone found her. I guess that is why my mother always talked about grandpa so much and not grandma. I wished I had listened to my mother more when she tried to speak to me. I wished I had told her and my father I cared when I had the chance, now all I could do was just sit and watch them.

Late one night, I was sitting looking out my bedroom window. A woman surrounded in light was in the yard.

"Grandma!" I ran down into the yard. It was not my grandmother.

The woman looked at me, "Bobby, would you like to cross over now? If you follow me, I will show you the way." Something was not right. It didn't feel right to me.

"Who are you?" I asked.

"I was sent here for you. I was sent to have you perform one task for me, and I will lead you to your salvation."

I started to follow the woman, and I looked at her, "No. I need to stay here with my mother. I need to make sure she is ok. She needs me."

The woman replied to me, "You will not get another chance, Bobby. This will be it. I can lead you to salvation."

I told her, "I will take my chances here."

The woman vanished before my eyes. I found it strange that I was a ghost, and I was being haunted. Haunted by people that I had never met. It seemed that death was just as confusing as life, maybe even more so. It would not be the last visit I would receive.

Chapter 4

The Man in Black

I was outside watching my father cook hamburgers on his grill, and I noticed a man dressed in a black suit waving at me. I walked over toward the man, and he smiled at me.

"Hello, Bobby," the man said.

"What do you want?" I asked.

"Straight to the point, I like that. I am here to let you know that everything is not always as it seems. I cannot give you any other help or advice, but this. You are doing what you feel is right, and that is the right thing to do. Remember one other thing, nobody sent here from the Lord will ever ask you for anything."

The man smiled again, turned, and walked away. I followed him, and as he rounded a corner, he was gone. I thought about what the man had told me. The lady in white had asked me to perform a task for salvation, and now this man was telling me that the Lord would not ask anything of me. I was confused. This was not like making a decision of the college I would attend, this was a decision for eternity, and apparently, there are people here that will lie to me as well.

I decided to go to my church, the church I grew up going to, so that I may find some peace and be able to think. I walked toward the church, and the feeling of calm and peace came over me the closer I got. I walked in and sat toward the back of the church. I sat there for hours. I was able to sit at the church through afternoon Mass, and I listened carefully to Father's words. I found it strange that Father had talked about how there were things that tempt us every day. He ended his sermon with the words, "Beware of the wolf that is dressed in sheep's clothing." That message stuck in my head. It reminded me of the woman that had visited me and asked me to perform a task. It reminded me of what the man in black had told me. I decided that I would go home and spend a final night with my parents, and I would then decide it was time to find my way to the Lord. I walked toward my house, and the man in black was sitting on the front steps of my house.

I looked at him and asked, "Are you back to tell me something else?"

"I am. I am here to take you to your grandmother. She is waiting for you."

I thought for a moment, "I thought I would have to decide where I would spend eternity?"

The man said, "You have. You traveled to your church and decided that it was time for you to move on. You renewed your faith, and now it is time to go. I need you to do something for me first."

I felt very uneasy. "What is it that you would ask me to do?"

The man in black replied, "I need you to have faith in me, have faith that I will deliver you to the place you need to be."

I looked at the man, and I spoke, "I will not follow you anywhere. You are not the same man that I talked to earlier, and I am sure that wherever it is you want me to follow, it isn't going to be good."

The man looked me right in the eyes, "You are a stubborn boy. I cannot waste any more time on you."

"Then don't. I will not see you again… I am not asking you, I am telling you."

The man sunk into the ground before my eyes into a black puddle and disappeared.

I walked into the house, and my mother was sitting on the couch, waiting for my father to come home from work. She had a strange smile on her face as if she would finally be ok. I kissed her on her head and said, "Goodbye, Mom, I will always be with you."

I turned around, and there was the beautiful woman that had asked my forgiveness before.

"Grandma? Is it time?"

The woman answered, "Yes, Bobby, it is time. I am here like I told you, I am here to take you home."

I asked her why all of the visits from the other angels. She told me that they were not angels, but agents of the dark realm. It is their job to try and trick souls that are unsure to follow them. She explained that she had been tricked herself, and when she chose to save the five people instead of her grandson, her soul was saved from the dark realm.

"What is the dark realm?" I asked.

My grandmother explained that it is where souls go when they are not sure of where they need to be. It is not Hell, but it brings you about as close to there as you ever want to be. She explained that because she had taken her own life, she was pulled there by the same man in black that had tried to get me to follow. He told her that she had to save me so she could bring herself to salvation.

"I knew that it was a sin to take my own life, but I also knew that I was not an angel and that only through forgiveness from one of my family members would save me. When I asked for your forgiveness for not saving you, it was not from the accident as it may have sounded. It was because I had never met you that I needed your forgiveness. If I had not left your mother, I might have been there to guide you, instead of finding you after you had died."

"So, I would have died either way?"

My grandmother answered, "Yes. I whispered into the man's ear to slow down, and he heard me. Otherwise, that family would have died too. The forgiveness I asked for was for not being there to help you in the first place. I crossed after I asked you because I repented for my sin, and listened to the voices that had been calling to me from the day I had died."

My grandmother explained many things to me, and it was now clear that lost souls were not safe even after death. I was thankful that I had listened to the man in black that had first visited me, and I wondered who he was. As we left for the gates of my salvation, I recognized the man in black at the gates, it was my grandfather. He was once again young, and it was he that had visited me the first time and gave me the advice that saved my soul. I return to the little house any time I want, often with my grandparents, to check in on my mother and father. I prepare for the day that I will meet them at the end of their earthly journey. I will be there to lead them home.

PART VII

The Ghost Lights

Chapter 1

Vacation

We were driving for our annual family vacation, making great time traveling the interstate at night. My wife and little girl were sleeping, and I was beginning to feel tired myself. I looked up at a sign, and the next exit was about 12 miles further. As the lines in the road raced past my mirror, the heavier my eyes began to feel. My head started to nod, and I must have fallen asleep. I felt the car swerve, and I grabbed the wheel fast and hard. I brought the car back under control and turned to my wife, "Ellen?" I said. I looked to my left, and my wife was gone. I turned and looked into the back seat, and my daughter was gone as well. I slammed on the brakes and brought the car to a screeching halt. "Ellen! Paige! Where are you!" I screamed.

I frantically opened all of the car doors and even the trunk, but I was alone. I hit my knees, "Ellen! Paige! Where are you?" I wept as I placed my face into my hands. I sat there for about half an hour, no cars or trucks passed, nobody else was out here but me. I was utterly alone. The only sound I could hear was the hum of the engine in my car as it idled away, waiting for me to jump in and move on down the road. I looked around again and called out once more. There was still no answer from my wife or my daughter. I got into my car and grabbed my cell phone to find that it had no service. I tried the radio, and there must have been no reception because all I heard was static. I was distraught. Where in the Hell did they go? Where the Hell did everybody go? I looked at the clock on my cell phone, and it said 3:28 a.m. I waited and walked around the car in disbelief. I guess maybe I was waiting for someone to come along, or for them to come walking up the road. It didn't happen. Nobody came, and Ellen and Paige did not return to me. It was me, out here, and I was alone.

I got into the still-running car and decided I would drive to the next exit and call the police. I could remember the sign back on the road before I dozed off said 12 miles. It shouldn't take that long to travel 12 miles and find a working phone. I put my seatbelt on, placed the car in drive, and placed the pedal to the floor. I figured if I got stopped by the police, I didn't have to find a phone then. The engine roared as I looked down at the speedometer. 95 mph, I should be at that exit within 3 minutes at this rate, I thought. I drove and drove and drove. It seemed as though a half hour had passed, and there was no sign of an exit. No sign of another vehicle. No sign of another person. I picked up my cell phone once more. 3:28 a.m. "What the Hell?" I asked out loud. I tried to dial my wife's number. There was still no service. I tried to dial 911. There was still no service. I tried the car radio once more, again there was only static.

I slammed on the brakes hard. The car nearly flew off of the road as the tires squealed under the force of the brakes. The car rocked from side to side and then rested at a complete stop as I looked down the dark highway. I had just driven for at least 30 minutes. I passed nobody, I saw no exits, and according to my cell phone, not 1 minute had passed. I sat in the middle of the highway and stared into the darkness past my headlights. "What in the Hell is going on?" I thought as I sat there listening to the idle of the engine of the car. I placed the car back in the park, and I opened the door and got out once again. I walked around the car, I looked at the tires, and I checked the bumpers to make sure I hadn't hit anything. The car was perfect. It sat there and idled, and the headlights burned into the darkness down the highway. I started to walk down the road into the beams of the headlights. I arrived at the edge of the visible light and peered into the darkness. There was nothing. Nothing but the road. Nothing but darkness. No vehicles, no exits, No Ellen or Paige. Nothing.

Chapter 2

Driving Into Eternity

I stood in the beams of the headlights for what seemed to be hours. Staggering back to the car, I reached in and grabbed my cell phone. 3:28 a.m. Not a minute had passed. It then dawned on me to look at the clock in the car. I jumped into the driver seat and peered hopefully at the clock on the dashboard. The illuminated numbers glowed 3:28 as the engine idling was the only sound I heard.

"I don't fricking believe this!" I said out loud. "What the Hell is going on? Where am I?" No answers presented themselves as I sat and stared at a clock on the dashboard of my car that would not advance to the next minute. I became enraged. I slammed the car door and violently shifted the car into drive. The car began to quickly accelerate as the lines on the highway began to rocket past me. The car's tachometer was all the way into the red, and I just left the pedal on the floor. If I blew the engine, then so be it. It wasn't like I was going to get passed 3:28 a.m. or find the next exit anyhow. I drove with the pedal pushed to the floor for at least an hour. I finally let up on the gas and removed my foot from the pedal, as the car continued to slow.

It slowed until finally, it was creeping down the road at the speed that the idled engine would carry it. Placing my foot onto the brake, I brought the car to a complete stop. Shifting the lever into

135

park, I sat there in disbelief that the clock on the dashboard still read 3:28. I checked my cell phone, and it too read 3:28 a.m. Not an exit had appeared, and not a moment had passed. The car sat and idled perfectly even after I had driven it harder than I ever had before. There was no way or reason that the engine shouldn't have blown up after running it that hard for over an hour. But yet, it idled perfectly, and no time had passed.

I returned to the car, and I released the trunk once again. I took out the tire iron I kept in there, and I began to stroll around the car. My walk became pacing back and forth in the headlight beams as I stared at the idling vehicle. I began to beat the hood of the car as I screamed the names of my wife and daughter. I busted out both of the headlights and dented the hood as I continued to swing the tire iron relentlessly. I busted out each window and shattered the windshield. I reached in, turned the car off, and whipped the keys into the darkness surrounding the road. I heard the tire iron bounce off the cement as I dropped it and began to run into the darkness down the road.

The moon shined bright enough for me to see the lines of the road as I ran out of breath, and my run quickly became a walk. I stopped and turned back to see the reflection of my now wrecked vehicle in the moonlight. I turned back and continued to walk away and over the next hill on the road. Turning around again, I could no longer see my car glisten in the light of the moon. I walked for what seemed to be an hour, and as I topped another hill down the highway, I could hear the idle of another car in the darkness ahead of me. My walk became faster and then turned into a flat out sprint as taillights appeared in the distance. As I approached the tail lights of the running vehicle, I noticed the driver's side car door was open. My run slowed, and I came to a complete stop as it became clear to myself that I was looking at my own car.

I walked around and peered in disbelief as I encircled the vehicle. Not a scratch. Not a dent. I reached in, and there on the passenger seat was my cell phone. As I reached into the car to check the phone, I reluctantly saw the time on the clock. It was still 3:28 a.m. In all the time I spent running away from this car, I made no progress in escaping it. I spun my body around, and I sat in the driver seat of the car. Placing my head onto the steering wheel, and I began to feel hopeless. I lifted my head, put the car in drive, and drove off into the night. I passed no exits. I saw no other vehicles. There was nothing but me, my car, and my cell phone that wouldn't place calls, and it wouldn't let another minute pass. I drove into the night, and I began to feel like I might be driving into eternity.

Chapter 3

Am I In Hell?

I began to think I was in an episode of some science fiction show. My thoughts went to driving with my family, and how we were on our way to our dream vacation. Now I had nothing but a car that wouldn't carry me another mile down the road, and a cell phone that wouldn't place a call or let time pass. I rolled down the window and threw the cell phone out. I began to stare at the speedometer as the car moved faster and faster down the highway. I felt more hopeless as the lines on the road moved faster past my car. The lines began to almost look like one solid yellow line as I looked, and the speedometer of the car was buried. I was easily going over 120 mph. I could feel the car move over the hills, and I could feel the engine roar as I continued into the darkness. What could I do to get out of the Hell I now suffered? What could I do to end the torment I felt as the car carried me faster and faster to nowhere.

I turned the headlights off and clutched the steering wheel as I waited for the car to either leave the road or slam into something as it traveled. It was at that moment over the horizon, I noticed something that wasn't there before. Lights. Into the dark night, over the horizon, the glow of a city, or truck stop, or something. I slowed the car, and I turned the headlights back on. I could feel hope fill my heart as I continued to drive toward the glow of lights.

It meant that my nightmare drive may soon come to an end. It meant that I may now be able to make a phone call. It meant that now I could try and find Ellen and Paige. It felt to me as though 8 hours had passed by. I had driven for hours, I had trashed my car, and I had traveled down the road of complete despair. Now there was hope. Now I could see the brilliance of lights. I topped the next hill, and the next, and the next. As I drove faster and faster, longer and longer, the lights continued to glow in the distance. A distance that never seemed to become shorter.

My journey towards the lights, and of hope, slowly became once again, a journey of despair. The lights never became anything more than a glow over the horizon that continued to elude and taunt me. I began to think that I was in Hell. I had to be. I looked again at the clock on the dashboard, and still, the time was the same. 3:28 was etched into that clock. It was etched into my memory. It was the moment of eternity that I would never be able to drive out of. It was the moment that I lost everything. It was the moment that my life became unbearable. It was the moment that all hope left my heart and mind, and in return, all I had was my car and the cell phone that I threw out of the window.

I continued to drive toward the glow. I thought of something new. I thought if I counted the seconds... one thousand one, one thousand two... if I counted to 60, that would be a minute. If I did that 60 times, that would be an hour. If I concentrated on the road, and counting, I would beat this clock. I would know for myself that this clock was lying to me. I would see for myself that time was indeed passing. I began to laugh out loud, "I beat you! I beat you... you goddamn timekeeper!" I finally had figured out a way to make sure the clock was lying about the time. I began to count. One thousand one, one thousand two, one thousand three; I counted this way to 60 one time after another until I had done it 60 times. Finally, I stopped the car and got out.

I danced around the car, taunting the clock on the dashboard. "I beat you! You lying bastard! I beat you! I just passed an hour!" The clock glowed back the numbers that never changed. 3:28 was still there. Never changing, never different. 3:28 was stuck as the time on that clock, and there wasn't a damn thing I could think of to make it any different. "Oh yeah?" I asked out loud as I punched the clock repeatedly, "Tell me the time now you piece of shit! Tell me now!" I screamed as the light of the clock was now gone, and I felt the blood dripping from my broken knuckles. "Looks like I won this round," I said as I looked up and continued to drive on. The lines on the road continued to whiz by, and still, there were no other vehicles and no exits. There was no sign of Ellen or Paige. There was also no longer a clock or cell phone to taunt me with the concept of time anymore.

DAN NORVELL

Chapter 4

Lost

I began to think to myself that I had lost my mind. I was talking to a car and a clock. I felt like the clock was a constant reminder that my existence would be forever frozen at 3:28. I was glad that it was gone. The reality of the pain in my hand reminded me that it was real. I could feel my knuckles swell, and the blood drip off of them as I rested my hand in the seat beside me. I drove on into the night and began to wonder if I was dreaming. "Is this a dream? Will I wake up in our bed with Ellen? What is going on here?" I thought to myself as I drove toward the glow of the ghost lights over the horizon that I couldn't seem to reach. I felt lost. Lost in time, lost in eternity. I would never see my wife or daughter again. I would never see another morning. All I would see is a broken line that continued to pass my car that traveled nowhere, and a night that would never end. I knew that if the clock was still there, it would still read 3:28. I was sure of it. Or was I? Why did I break the clock? Why did I throw my cell phone out the window? What if they did change? What if maybe they would have changed if I had just waited a moment longer?

I tried to remember what color the numbers were on the clock that was no longer there. I think they were the same as the digital numbers on the odometer. The odometer! Am I traveling any distance? I started to watch the odometer as the miles added by one each minute that I continued to drive. "Let me think, I got the oil changed before we left and drove home. We left for the trip the next morning, and that was 1000 miles ago. The sticker they put on my windshield read 32,342, and now I had 28,973 miles on the odometer. I have traveled another 600 miles!" The last time I saw my wife and daughter, we were only about 200 miles from home. So, even though I cannot seem to pass the time, I can travel distance. If I can travel distance, I should eventually make it to those ghost lights.

I continued to drive as I watched the miles add one at a time to the odometer of my car. I felt hopeful once more that I would see my family again. I looked down, and a thought crossed my mind, "Gas! What if I run out of gas?" I quickly looked at the gas gauge, and it still read full. Not one gallon had been used, and I had traveled at least 800 miles since the last time I put gas into the car. I started to try and think about things from a scientific standpoint, "If time doesn't pass, then maybe my gas won't burn." That was crazy. The engine has been running the entire time. The only time it wasn't running was when I beat the car with the tire iron. I began to think that maybe this wasn't really my car. I stopped the car, opened the glove box, and pulled out the registration and insurance card. It read, "Jack K. Kirby. 5708 Kings Way." It was my car, alright.

As I placed the papers back into the glove box, I realized that my hand had quit bleeding, and it no longer hurt. I looked down to see that it was completely healed. As I stared at my hand, I reached up and turned off the dome light. There was a soft glow coming from the dashboard. I slowly turned my head and looked at 3:28, softly glowing at my face. At that same moment, I looked over toward the odometer and checked the numbers, and calculated the miles I had traveled since the oil change. I had only traveled 1000 miles, the last 600 miles were gone.

I placed the gear shifter into park and got out of the car. "Why, God? What have I done to deserve this?" I wailed. I placed my face into my hands and began to cry as I thought that maybe I had fallen asleep at the wheel, had died, and was now in Hell. It could be the only explanation. Was I trapped, or was I lost? I thought Hell was fire and brimstone. I thought the devil himself would have found me by now and took my soul for his own. There was no fire, and there was no brimstone. There was a car engine humming and headlights shining into the darkness of a road that I would never exit off of. There was a clock on the dashboard that would never advance from 3:28 to 3:29. There were no other vehicles and no family. There were no miles on the car, and there was no hope of ever getting to the ghost lights over the horizon that endlessly glowed in the distance. I hadn't used a single drop of gasoline, and to me, it seemed as if miles and hours had passed.

I sat and leaned my back against the car and listened to the hum of the engine that would never quit. I thought of my beautiful little girl and my wife that I would never see again. I wondered if the same thing happened to everybody that died. I felt complete anguish as I began to pray to God for a miracle. "Dear God, please. I am not a praying man, but I need to know if Paige and Ellen are at least with you. Please, God, dear Christ, give me a sign." I began to weep again as I heard a familiar sound coming from inside of the car. I jumped up and reached for where the sound was coming from. I opened the glove box, and there was my cell phone. It wasn't broken on the side of this endless highway somewhere in the darkness. It was in my glove box, and it was ringing.

Chapter 5

The Way Home

I picked up the cell phone and looked at the number. The number across the screen was all sevens. I answered the phone and heard a voice I hadn't heard in years. I listened carefully as the voice told me 6 words, "Have Faith, Go to the light."

"How?" I asked. "How do I go to the light? Dad? Dad!"

The voice was gone. All that was left was dead air. I was perplexed. I had just received a phone call from my father, and he told me to have faith and continue on toward the light. I hadn't heard his voice in so long. The thing that was so strange to me was that my Dad had been dead for over 10 years. If my Dad was going to call me on my cell phone and tell me to go to the light, then I was damn well going to go to those lights.

I got back into the car and placed it in the drive. The broken lines again seemed to become one continuous line as I passed 100 mph and climbing. I kept scanning into the headlight beams looking for a sign that I was getting closer to something. All at once, lightning flashed across the sky and filled it with light. I could feel my chest tighten with every lightning flash as I pushed the car to go faster and faster. My arms began to tingle as I gripped the steering wheel harder as the car thundered down the highway. I suddenly felt revived, as I could see the lights over the horizon actually seem to become brighter. I felt the excitement grow as I topped the next hill, and the lights were now clear to me.

It was apparent that I was now traveling toward answers as I noticed the clock on the dashboard read 3:29. Time had now passed for me. The glow of the lights became brighter and brighter as I roared towards them. The closer I got, the easier it was to see that I was coming to the lights of an exit. I could feel the car begin to sputter as I passed an exit sign that read "Home 1 mile". I thought, "just 1 more mile car." The lightning became more intense as the car began to slow. I saw steam begin to pour out from under the hood as the engine made a loud bang and the car slowed to a halt. I looked at the clock, and it now read 3:30.

I put the car in park and opened the door and began to run as fast as I could toward the exit. It was about a quarter of a mile away, and the lightning was intense. I could see the sky light up as I ran faster. I finally reached the exit ramp and began to run up it. I saw a brilliant flash of light as lightning hit me, and everything went completely dark. I could feel I was on my back as I began to open my eyes. I heard a little voice and felt a hand holding mine as I turned my head and looked.

"Daddy?"

"Paige?" I said. "Where is Mommy?"

"She is over in that bed, Daddy. She'll be ok. She told me to come and check on you."

My daughter told me as she tightened her grip onto my hand. I later learned from my wife that we had been in an accident and veered off of the road. We were brought to the hospital, and I had died on the operating table at 3:28 a.m. The doctors had to work on me and shock my heart several times to bring me back.

I shook my head in disbelief. I kept telling my wife how sorry I was for wrecking our car and vacation. I was so happy to be alive and not alone. A week later, I was released from the hospital, and we traveled home so I could recover and return to work in the next few weeks. I finally told my wife of the experience I had while I was dead, and how I thought I was going to lose my mind wherever I was. Our life returned to normal, and the accident soon became a memory. About a year later, I was lying in bed, and our phone began to ring. I rubbed my eyes and looked over at the numbers on the clock radio beside our bed. 3:28 a.m. I reached over, answered the phone, and heard a voice on the other end of the line. It told me, "You were never alone." The voice was my Dad's.

PART VIII

Dead Time

DAN NORVELL

Chapter 1

Investigation

I couldn't wait to get to that old abandoned hospital. Cassie, Bill, and I had planned and talked about it for months. I finally purchased that Ultraviolet camera and a new voice recorder just for this investigation. The three-hour drive could not go fast enough, but at least we had enough time to discuss the investigation. We would stay together, and we would do EVP sessions in the old morgue and the emergency room of the hospital. We finally arrived and parked the car about three blocks from the entrance. It was dusk, and we had arrived just in time to do a walk around the outside perimeter of the hospital.

"Hey, Bill. I found a place that we can sneak in after sunset."

"That is awesome, Leslie. Let me set up the trap camera here, and we will pick it up when we sneak back out this way." Bill replied.

"Ok, Bill. And after we finish, you get to buy breakfast at that little truck stop on the way back home." Cassie teased Bill.

We continued walking around the outside of the hospital while we waited for the sun to set completely. The building was so enormous, it covered a whole city block. Signs were hanging everywhere that warned of the dangers of entering an abandoned building. Still, we had done this dozens of times, and we needed some new pictures to post on our team's website. We took photos of the outside of the hospital, and I took a picture of Bill and Cassie standing in front of the Emergency Room ambulance entrance. After taking their picture, Bill shattered the entrance window so we could enter there.

"I want to do an EVP session inside of the trauma room down there, Bill," I said. "Can you imagine all of the poor people that were snapped out of the living world in that room?"

"With as many years that this hospital saw action in this city, I think thousands of people died in there, Leslie," Bill replied.

We broke a light stick, settled our gear onto the floor, and took out our video camera and voice recorders. I began to ask questions, and the feeling in the room became very heavy.

"Is anybody with us? Did you die here?"

Out of the darkness, as clear as day, we all heard, "Yes." I could feel the hair on the back of my neck stand up. I looked at Cassie, and I could tell that she was unnerved as well. Bill sat there with his eyes wide, "I heard that answer just like they were standing right here!"

"I know! This hospital is awesome! We have only been here for about an hour, and we are already getting responses!" I said gleefully. "Let's play back the recorder to see if we caught anything else."

"Ok. You're the boss Leslie." Bill said as he picked up the recorder. We played back the recording, and we heard the answer to my question. As we listened to the initial response, the voice then warned us, "You will die here too." We all stood and stared at that recorder in astonishment.

"Did that voice just say what I think it said?" Bill asked us.

"I think so, Bill," I said. "You know what guys, suddenly I don't feel well. My stomach is turning."

"Leslie? Are you ok? Do you want to leave?" Cassie asked me as she rubbed my back.

"No. We came here to find ghosts, and that EVP session was a great start." I said. "Grab our gear and set up a trap camera here. We will pick it up when we head back out."

"Leslie, maybe we should just go. I am feeling really strange about being here now." Bill told me.

"Bill! You are always the one coaxing me to stay longer! You're just creeped out from the voice on the recorder, aren't you?" I asked him.

"Yes. We have never caught a voice that told us we would die before. Maybe we should heed the warning." Bill replied as his voice trembled.

"Bill, we did not save up and drive three hours to stay in the best place we have ever investigated for only one hour. Relax, we'll be fine. Nothing is gonna happen to any of us." I reassured him.

We set our next trap camera in the trauma room, and we moved on. I could hear Cassie and Bill whispering as we walked through the dark hallways that seemed to go on forever.

"Guys, come on! We have been waiting for this." I told them.

"I know Leslie, but I have a horrible feeling about moving on," Bill said. "You told us once that if we were ever feeling negative that we would all leave then and there. We are now breaking that rule."

"Ok, guys. I'll tell you what, I wanna see the morgue and take pictures in it with the new UV camera. Let's do that, and we will head out of here." I told them. "Agreed?"

"Agreed," Cassie answered reluctantly. "We need to make it quick Leslie, I have to agree with Bill, something isn't right tonight."

"You are both spooked, and it has put you off of your game. I'll go down to that morgue alone if you guys are too scared." I snapped at them.

"Nobody goes alone, Leslie. It is all or none, your rules, not ours." Bill said. "If you are going to make rules, you have to abide by them as well. Let's go get your pictures and get out of here."

"Now, you're talking. That's the Billy, I know!" I said as I patted him on the shoulder. We continued deeper into the hospital and searched for the morgue.

DAN NORVELL

Chapter 2

Carelessness

We searched for the morgue for an hour, traveling through a maze of corridors and stairwells. It felt like the longer we stayed in the hospital, the more the hospital seemed to come to life. It was quite a while before Bill spoke up, "Leslie, that's it. We have wandered through here for almost two hours now! It is time to get the heck out of here."

"Come on, you guys. Are you going to really do this now? We have to be close by now. Give me another half hour, if we don't find that morgue, we can get out of here." I begged them.

"No, Leslie," Cassie said. "That's it. We need to go now. If you aren't going to admit we are in over our head here, then I am. There is something about this place, we need to go, and we need to do it now."

"You guys go then. I'm gonna take pics in that morgue." I told them. I was angry. I looked them both in the eyes, "I am going up around that corner, if it isn't there, we go. Wait right here and keep your light on me."

"That's not a good idea, Leslie. Wait up." Bill said as I heard them begin to chase after me. I took another step, and the floor was gone. I fell down, and my neck popped, and I felt something go through my back and out of my stomach.

"Leslie!" I heard Bill and Cassie scream as their lights hit me in the face.

"Oh, my God!" Cassie screamed as she looked down at me. "Leslie, we're coming. Just stay still!"

I could hear them frantically trying to find their way down to me. I felt around, and my stomach was wet. I picked my hand up, and it was completely covered with blood. I tried to call out to Bill and Cassie, but I couldn't. They finally made it to my side, and Cassie was crying. "Leslie! Leslie! Answer me!" She screamed. Bill was calling 911 on his cell phone, and I could hear the voice through the phone, answering him.

I watched Cassie become more frantic by the second as she kept trying to get me to talk to her. I was exhausted, and I kept looking into Cassie's eyes. "I'm sorry," I tried to tell her as I put my hand on her face. I watched as the blood from my hand stained her face as I touched her. "Put pressure on it, Cassie!" Bill screamed as he held the phone in his hand. "She is dying right here! Hurry!" He yelled into the phone. I removed Cassie's hand from my stomach and held it with mine. I continued to look into her eyes as I heard sirens coming closer from a distance. I only closed my eyes for a second, but I could hear many voices in the room I had fallen into. When I opened them again, I saw firemen and police everywhere. I could hear Bill telling them what had happened as Cassie cried. I could no longer make sense of anything they were saying. I felt them move me, and I could feel the blood pour out of my back as they did. I kept focused on Cassie as everything became dark. The last thing I heard was a faint whisper in my ear, "I tried to tell you that you would die here."

Chapter 3

Awakening

I opened my eyes, and there was moonlight shining through the cracks in the wall of the old hospital. "What just happened?" I thought to myself as I looked all around. I called out into the darkness, "Bill? Cassie? Where are you guys?" Where are all of the firemen and police? I felt around on the ground for my flashlight. The ground felt dry. Maybe I had fallen and hit my head, and this was all just a dream. I finally found my flashlight, and I clicked it on. I was still inside of the hospital, and I was alone. I felt my stomach, but there was no blood. "Did I imagine all of this? Is somebody messing with my mind?" I wondered.

I began to move down the hallway I woke up in. Shining the light through the cracks in the walls, none of them were big enough to squeeze myself through. The best choice now would be to look for my friends and try to find a way out of here, but I was confused by what I had just experienced. Was that going to happen to me if I ignored the warning from the EVP? I kept walking down the hallway as it seemed to go on forever. I felt around for my camera, it should still have been hanging around my neck, but wasn't there. All I had was my flashlight.

I finally came to an area where the hallway broke into four separate ways. I found a sign on the wall with an arrow that pointed the way to the emergency room. If I followed the arrows toward the emergency room, I could collect our trap cameras, and get out of here. Entering the ER, I looked around with my flashlight and found it was just as dirty and abandoned as it was earlier tonight when we arrived.

I began to search for the trap cameras we placed, but I couldn't find them. I yelled out into the darkness again for Cassie and Bill, but I couldn't hear an answer. I found my way to the window that Bill had broken for us to get in. Once there, I would leave the hospital, return to the car, grab my cell phone, and call Bill. I finally arrived at the window, but it was completely boarded up. I shined my light out of the unbroken window. The grass outside a lot taller than when we walked in here tonight. I turned around and thought, nothing seemed to look the same now.

I yelled as loud as I could, "Bill! Cassie! C'mon guys! Jokes over! Bill! Let's go home now!" The only thing I heard was the rain start to hit the window glass next to the boards that held me inside of the hospital. I walked away from the window and back toward the trauma room where we had heard the voice. "Is there anybody in here?" I asked as I heard footsteps in the hallway. "Bill?" I looked all around and saw nobody. "Bill! Cassie!" I screamed at the top of my lungs. I heard footsteps behind me again, but they were coming from inside of the trauma room now. Feeling uneasy, I entered the room and scanned it with my flashlight but saw nothing. I felt as if there was a presence here with me that I couldn't see. "Is anybody here?" I asked.

"I am here." A voice answered.

Chapter 4

Helping the Dead

I was utterly horrified. "Who is that? Show yourself!" I shouted as I scanned the room with my flashlight over and over.

"I cannot show myself. If I could, I would."

"Who is saying that?" I asked as I stood there, trembling.

"My name was Nathan. I died here. I was the one that talked to you on the night you asked if anybody was here."

"You're a ghost?" I asked.

"I guess I am." The voice replied to me.

"How are you talking to me? It is as if we are just having a normal conversation."

"I am not sure. I cannot see you. I can only hear you. Just as you cannot see me." The voice said.

"Can you see my flashlight?" I asked as I turned it on.

"I can. I just cannot see you. I can hear you very clearly now, though. It is nice to talk with somebody after so many years." The voice told me.

"Years? How long have you been dead?" I asked.

"I am not sure. I was shot in the line of duty. I stood right here in this room as my wife held my hand while I died. I watched my son kiss my cheek as he told me goodbye. It was an everlasting torment." The voice answered.

"I am Leslie. I am a paranormal investigator. I help the dead." I told him. "I am amazed that you and I are having this conversation. I cannot wait until Bill and Cassie hear about this. It is truly amazing." I told the voice.

"How do you help the dead, Leslie? What can you do to help?"

"I can help you cross over. I can help you find your way to heaven." I told him.

I was so excited. This was the exact proof that we had been searching for. I now had evidence of life after death without question. I was speaking with the spirit of a dead police officer, and he was answering me with intelligent answers. It was the most fantastic thing that we were just talking.

"Can I call you Nathan?"

"Of course, you can. That is my name." He answered.

"Nathan? What year is it? Do you remember?" I asked him.

"It is 1965. I was on duty with my partner, and we had just surprised a guy that was robbing a gas station. The guy turned around and shot me in the chest. My partner shot the man, and he held his hand over my chest until they finally got me here to this room. The doctors worked to try and save my life for a long time as I stood behind them and watched. It was all very strange, Leslie. What year is it now?"

"I am so sorry, Nathan. The year is 2009." I told him.

"2009?" His voice trembled, "I have been dead for almost thirty years! My son is older than I was when I died by now. Oh, my God! Why have I been forsaken to this?"

"Nathan?" I asked him softly, "Did you see a light anywhere in the room when you died? A white light, maybe?"

"I think so. I felt as if I was being pulled toward it. I didn't go to it because I wanted to see my son. That day was the last time I had ever seen him."

"It's ok, Nathan. I will try and help you. Did you know that you died at the time?" I asked.

"No. I thought I was dreaming. Everything seems like a dream since then. I cannot believe that you said the year is 2009. It seems like it has only been a year to me."

"I know it is hard to believe Nathan. Do you want peace? Do you want to go and be where you can have it?"

"I really didn't realize I was dead until the night you were here with your friends. I knew I was dead for sure when they wheeled that girl out of here. I knew because I stood in their way, and they walked through me. I always thought I might be dead, but I wasn't sure."

"Nathan, you need to go now. You need to cross over and pass into the light. It is ok now."

"Why couldn't I go before Leslie? Why?" He asked me.

"Sometimes, people need to realize they are dead, Nathan. You now realize this. Go now." I told him as a light began to form in the corner of the room.

I could see Nathan now and what he looked like in life. He was still wearing his uniform. He smiled as he walked toward the light that grew brighter by the second. He turned and smiled at me, "Leslie. Come with me." He said.

"I can't, Nathan, I am not dead," I said.

"Goodbye. Thank You." He said as he waved and disappeared into the light. The room became dark once more, and I was now alone. I had just experienced one of the greatest moments anyone ever could. I hit the ground and cried as I realized I had just freed a tortured soul from his prison.

DAN NORVELL

Chapter 5

Who's Here?

I still was in complete disbelief as I tried to take in everything that I had just witnessed. I could not wait until I could tell Bill and Cassie about it. Once I found them, I would explain the events of what had taken place in detail. We would place the story on our website with pictures of the hospital. I was so excited; I could hardly contain myself as I walked the hallways yelling out to Bill and Cassie. I continued my search, and as I did, I could hear voices coming from below me. I found my way to a stairwell and made my way downstairs. I could hear the voices getting closer. It had to be Bill and Cassie.

I called out, "Bill! Cassie! Here I am. I'm coming." I walked into a clearing, and five people were standing there with equipment. They were doing what appeared to be an EVP session.

"Hello," I called toward them. "What team are you with?" I asked as I got closer to them.

"This is where she died. She was impaled on that rod that held the cement together over here. She fell through the hole in the floor above us." A man said as he shined his light onto a hole in the ceiling above us.

"What was her name, Chuck?" Another member of the group asked. I was curious. I had not heard this story about the hospital before.

"I can't remember Jake. She died, staring into her friend's eyes. It must have been horrible."

They all sat down and lit candles and began doing their session. "Is anybody here with us?" They asked.

"I am," I answered. "I am Leslie."

"Can you give us a sign that you are here?" They asked.

"Can I sit with you all for a minute? I am looking for my friends. Their names are Bill and Cassie." I asked them. I reached out and shook a girl in the group by the shoulder, and she screamed.

"Chuck! Something touched me!"

"Ok, That's enough for tonight. Let's get out of here." Chuck told the group.

They calmed the girl down as they walked to the spot that they must have entered the building. I followed along and tried to explain that I was just trying to see if they had seen my friends. They squeezed through a hole in the wall one by one as I stood and watched them leave. I wanted to follow, but something drew me back into the hospital. I turned my light on and continued my search for Bill and Cassie.

I searched the halls of the hospital for hours. I found it strange that the sun did not seem to be rising. Maybe I just thought that it had been longer than it actually was. I just wanted to find Bill and Cassie and explain the events of the night to them. I know they will be just as excited as I am about helping Nathan cross over. It was definitely the best part of the investigation. I wandered on and on throughout the hospital. I was starting to become worried about Bill and Cassie. I would never have guessed in a million years that they would have ever become separated from me.

I decided to sit for a few minutes and go through the events of tonight, so I could recount them onto our website. I couldn't wait to share with the field that I had interviewed and helped an actual spirit cross over. I sat there and rested for a while. I started to hear voices in the hallways. I heard voices that I recognized. It was Bill and Cassie! I had finally found them! What a story I had for them.

Chapter 6

Finding Out The Truth

I could hear the voices getting closer and closer. I recognized Bill's voice, and I could hear that they had other people with them. I rushed up the hallway, and I saw the light from their flashlights coming closer.

I shouted out to them, "Bill! Cassie! Here I am! I am so glad you're here!" I didn't hear them begin to run toward the sound of my voice or answer me. I could hear them talking, and I overheard them say that the spot was just around the corner. I stood and watched as Bill and Cassie came into sight with Chuck and Jake from earlier tonight. I stared at Bill in disbelief. He looked older and more cumbersome. Cassie looked different as well. I rubbed my eyes and peered at them harder. "Bill? Cassie? What happened to you? Where have you been?" I asked. My questions fell unto deaf ears.

Cassie looked terrified as she began to cry, "Bill, this is it." she said as they stopped in the same spot that those other guys were doing an EVP session earlier. "This is where it all happened. This is where we lost her."

I stepped up close, "Cassie, I am right here. I have been looking for you all night long."

Chuck and Jake played back to Bill and Cassie their EVP from earlier, "This is what we caught the night we were here." I could faintly hear my voice on the recorder. I heard it answer Chuck, "I am, I am Leslie." when he asked if anyone was here.

"I remember that night," Bill said. "She was looking for the morgue, and she fell into the hole above us. She fell onto the rebar rod over here, and we watched her bleed to death."

"I am not dead! What in the Hell are you all talking about? I am right here! I have been looking for you all night long! What in the Hell are you all talking about?" I wailed out, confused.

"She stared into my eyes as she died. She placed her hand on my face, and she tried to tell me she was sorry. Bill, I can't do this. I can't be here anymore." Cassie said.

I stumbled back, "It wasn't a dream? I'm dead? I died that night?" It all started to make sense to me now. The reason I could talk to Nathan, the reason he heard me, the reason all I seem to do is wander. The reason Nathan asked me to come with him into the light! "Oh, dear God! What have I done?"

"Leslie? Leslie, are you here?" Cassie asked. "Leslie, it is time to cross over. You are a good soul; you don't deserve to be stuck here. Go to the light."

"I can't, Cassie! I had the chance, and I didn't go! I didn't know I was dead!" I cried as I reached for her hand.

"My God!" Cassie said, "Bill! Something is touching my hand! Leslie! Is that you?"

"Yes, Cassie! It's me! I am stuck here! Help me, Cassie!" I cried.

"Let's pray for her, everybody," Cassie said as she led a prayer. "Please bring our sweet friend Leslie into your grace Lord." She said as I knelt and cried.

I prayed with them. I looked toward the end of the hallway as I noticed a light. Bill and Cassie saw the light as well. I heard a voice coming from the light, "Leslie. It's time to come home. You helped me, so I am here to help you now," Nathan said as he held his hand out toward me. I got up from my knees and walked toward the light.

I could hear Cassie say to Bill, "My God, do you see her? I can see her walking toward the light. Leslie, Keep going, Leslie. Go into the light."

I turned to see the tears running down Cassie and Bill's faces. Chuck and Jake stood and stared in amazement.

"We miss you, Leslie. Go be at peace. You proved that there is an afterlife," Cassie said.

I smiled at them and took Nathan's hand. I looked back at Cassie, "I'm sorry, Cassie. Thank You."

Cassie nodded, "You're welcome, Leslie. Goodbye."

I smiled as I felt the warmth of the light fill me, I watched as the darkness faded and swallowed up my friends. I turned to see Nathan leading me to my Mother and Father, waiting for me on the other side.

DAN NORVELL

PART IX

Dark Souls

Chapter 1

Revenge

After working late that night, I came home to a busted front door and blood all over the house. I ran into our bedroom, and on the bed, lay the body of my wife, shot in the head. I heard my son cry out, and I turned and ran to his room. A man standing over him with a gun whipped around and squeezed the trigger. I felt the bullet rip into my stomach and exit through my back. I hit the floor in anguish. I looked up to see the man throw a pillow over my son's face and squeeze off several rounds into my little boy. He then walked over and kicked me in the face.

"That should teach you to pay your debts, you piece of shit."

I got a good look at his face as he pulled the trigger once more. I remember the gun being aimed at my face, and then everything went black. The next thing I remember is my wife and son standing in a brilliant light, and my son was saying, "Daddy, come with us." The light disappeared, and I remained standing in a pool of my own blood. My lifeless body lay at my feet. I walked out of the house, and the man that ended my family's lives was on a cell phone.

"It's done, boss. 2575 Fifth Avenue."

I could hear a voice on the other end, "You damn idiot! The address was 2575 Fifth STREET. You just killed the wrong people!"

"Well, I guess I made a mistake, but I don't think that guy will complain about it." The voice on the other end of the line laughed, and so did the man.

"I'll go and take care of it right now, boss."

The man got into an expensive-looking car and drove off. I sat there on the front steps, shaking my head. My family was murdered over a wrong address, and these people couldn't care less. I was sickened and, if I still had a stomach, I would have been ill. I walked back into my house, and, by that time, the sun was rising. It appeared that this man had broken in, beat my wife, and dragged her all around the house before he shot her. I was filled with anger.

I dropped to my knees and cried out, "Why God? Why did this happen? I will give my soul for revenge!"

I heard a voice behind me, "Be very careful what you wish for, Victor." I turned and saw a man in a black cloak and hood, but I couldn't see his face.

"Who are you?" I asked with a shudder.

"I am the angel of death. I am a product of heaven to perform a function. I really am not an angel, I have no allegiance to heaven or Hell, I just perform a function, and my function is death, no matter how it comes to people."

"So, you were here just moments ago when my family was taken?"

"I was, and I took your lives." I tried to grab the man.

"You rotten son of a bitch!" I screeched. The man picked me up by the throat, and I felt as if I was being choked.

"Just because you are dead does not mean that I cannot inflict pain on your soul. Calm down." He set me down, and I looked at him while rubbing my throat.

"Where are my wife and son?"

"They have crossed over. Your anger and hatred are keeping you here. There is nothing you can do, Victor. I returned when I heard you offer your soul. You had better be thankful it was me that heard you and not one of the devil's minions."

"And what if it were?" I asked. "Would I be able to avenge the senseless deaths of the innocent lives?"

"No. You would have been tricked into losing your soul to Hell, and that would serve no purpose. You have been a good man

174

all of your life, and it seems that a strange twist of fate has brought us together." It was then and there that I struck a deal with the angel of death.

"Victor, I will grant your wish. You will work for me. The job is simple. You will see to it that people die. I have many that work with me, but your job will be special. You will kill those that have been evil. You will kill them and send them on their way to Hell."

"What's the catch?" I asked.

"The catch—you will belong to me. You will do the job I assign to you, and you will do it until I set you free to be with your family. That could be 100 years from now; it could never happen either. It will be the chance you have to take, and the choice is yours."

"I'll do it under one condition. I get to be the one that kills the ones responsible for my family dying."

"Agreed. And, after that, you kill for me. You kill no matter where the soul is bound for, and you kill on my command. It is an act of nature, Victor, and it will happen with or without you. Revenge will taint your soul. Be careful not to let it consume you for, if it does, your soul will have no salvation. It will find only despair in the pits of Hell."

"So, I kill without the threat of going to Hell?" I asked, trying to wrap my mind around the arrangement.

"You perform a necessary function, Victor. The Lord will not hold that against you. The first thing I grant you is your revenge. After that, you kill for me." I agreed to the deal, and my appearance changed. I was now wearing a black cloak of my own. I did not appear to be the same man that I was. I felt my face, and there was no longer flesh on it. I looked at the man and, for the first time, he looked at me. I was staring into the face of a skeleton.

"Now you look like me, Victor. There are some rules for our game. You cannot let everyone die peacefully in their sleep. If everyone dies that way, death no longer will be feared, and that fear helps to keep many people faithful. You will be able to use a gift I have given you—that if you think it, it will come to pass. So, if you want to take someone in a car accident for example, you can think of the gas pedal sticking or the brakes giving out or a heart attack behind the wheel, and it will happen."

"Anything else? I have some people I need to track down," I said impatiently.

"Patience, Victor. You now have eternity. You do not want to make it too easy on them with something quick now, do you? Victor, you will be seen by the deceased after you have killed them. It will be up to you to decide how you appear to them. You can look like you do now or like a nice old man, but you cannot reveal yourself before the deed is done. I will make one exception to this rule. You can reveal yourself to the man that killed you but, after that, never again before death."

"Why didn't I see you at the time of my death?" I asked.

"It is because I have made myself well accustomed to hiding in the shadows. It is time to start our work, Victor. You have to carry out your first assignment."

Chapter 2

Irony

It seemed that irony was already going to take a bite of me. The first person I was going to have to kill would be my mother.

"My mother?" I asked incredulously. "I thought I would oversee the evil people; my mother isn't evil!"

"You are correct. Your mother is not evil, but she will die this morning after hearing news of the act that took her family from her. It will be up to you to carry this out, Victor. It is the first lesson in the line of many you will come to know."

In an instant, we were at my mother's house. The phone was ringing, and I knew it would be the police calling. She never answered the phone. I paced the floor in her apartment, thinking to myself, "How much misery could my sisters take? They lost me, their nephew, their sister-in-law, and their mother all in one day." I didn't think I could do it.

The angel appeared, "What are you waiting for, Victor? This is what you wanted, is it not? Whether you do it or I do, your mother will die today. Remember what the rules are; they may be used to your advantage in this case."

There came a knock at my mother's door. I looked out, and it was the police. My mother went to the door, and the officers broke the news to her. I thought, "Heart attack." My mother started to breathe hard, and she grabbed her chest. She fell to the floor, and the officers called on their radios for an ambulance. I stood and watched my mother stand up from her body and look at me. She let out a blood-curdling scream and ran into her bedroom. I remembered that I looked like death but also that I could appear to her as anyone. I followed her into her room and appeared as myself.

"Mom, Mom... it's me. I have come to show you the way to heaven."

She looked up at me. "Victor? What was that? How are you here?" A brilliant light began to shine.

"Mother, you need to go. Walk into the light. I know that Dad is waiting for you."

"You aren't coming with me?" she asked.

"I am not, Mom. I will think of you all every minute of my existence, I promise."

I hugged my mother and sent her into the light. I started to think that I had made a mistake and that I should have crossed with my family. I looked at my mother's body on the floor and watched the officers working to save her life. The angel put his bony hand on my shoulder.

"Victor, you have done well, most could not have done it. If you look at it this way, it was a gift to you from me."

"How do you figure that you prick?" I spat through my grief.

"Name-calling will not get you any points, Victor. The gift was that it could have been another, and they could have made your mother suffer for a few hours. So it was your call, and she went out your way. That was my gift to you."

I didn't feel as though I had received any gift. I felt utterly horrible, and I wondered when I would have to take the life of another I loved because of my twisted deal.

"When do I get to exact my revenge?" I asked.

"I oversee all deaths, Victor. He shall be yours. I promised you that, and I will uphold my end of our bargain. I have a few more jobs for you to carry out, but they should be much easier for you.

"These people are Mexican drug lords. I want them to suffer before you take them, Victor. They do not deserve any mercy, for they show none."

In an instant, I was in a Mexican warehouse. I observed several men standing around, smoking cigars, and cigarettes. They were counting money and laughing about how the man they killed last night had screamed like a pig. All at once, I thought, "Massacre!" The Mexican police burst through the doors and opened fire. The men picked up their weapons and shot back. I walked up to one of the men, looked at him and thought, "Bullet through the head!" Instantly, a bullet hit him right between the eyes. He rose out of his body and looked at my skeletal face. He pointed and screamed.

I said, "Nobody can hear you, my evil friend. You have come to meet your death!" All at once, a black pit opened beneath the man. I am not sure what it belonged to, but the claw of what grabbed that man by the leg was a lot scarier than me, of that I was sure. That man screamed until the pit closed over the top of him.

I thought to myself, "Welcome to Hell, you cold-hearted bastard!" It seemed that revenge was being carried out by me, and these people were as deserving as any to receive my wrath. One by one, the drug lords fell. With a single thought, they died. They would die as I saw fit—a ruptured aorta, a headshot, whatever I could think of. That is the way they went and, each time, I observed that hideous claw grab them and take them to the pits of Hell. I actually enjoyed the deaths of these evil men. I saw another hooded figure on the side of the police. He had a gentle glowing face. He would hold onto the hands of the victims he claimed and help them into the light. I would see him make the sign of the cross as he sent them through.

After the moaning stopped and they were all dead and sent to the other side, I walked toward the other hooded figure.

"You must be the one that sends the good ones along," I said. The figure looked at me with tears streaming down his face.

"Hey, I know it is horrible, but it is a fact of life. Death will visit everyone," I said. His gentle eyes rested upon my empty sockets.

"I weep not for the souls that I have had to send to my Lord's kingdom, but for you. I weep for the lost soul you have become, Victor. Not even a day and the revenge that has filled you has made you enjoy the fact that the power you now possess can feed the thirst for your hopeless journey. I pity the soul that is being lost."

"Who was there to weep for my family? Who wept for my innocent little boy as a monster put bullets through his tiny head?

Save your tears for a soul that deserves them! I am finding my newfound power to be right where it needs to be," I responded, angrily.

The gentle-faced man looked at me, "Revenge will consume you. It will make you worse than the pit you are charged with overseeing. It will make you a brother to the Prince of Darkness himself. Do not let that happen, Victor. You may once again be reunited with that little boy, but not if revenge takes the place of the soul of the good man you once were."

"I will not be ashamed of the feeling it gives me to end the life of someone that deserves it. I will be the best dealer of death that I can be when it comes to taking evil people to meet in Hell," I told him.

"Then maybe you are already there yourself, Victor. May God protect the soul you have left." He was gone, and I looked around at the carnage. I felt my face crack as I smiled, "They deserved it." I looked forward to the next group of evil that I would introduce myself to, and I began almost to pity them. I pity them because I would become very good at the job I was given. It was the best job I ever had, and I would do it until I was able to meet, face-to-face, the man that had taken everything from me. What a glorious day that would be.

I found myself in the apartment of a man in New York City. He had just finished cutting the arm off a girl he had strangled and was drinking her blood! I looked at her little face. She couldn't have been more than 10. How I would take this lowlife out would be terrible, even to the angel that gave me the job.

Chapter 3

Show No Mercy

I watched the man drink the blood of that little girl and then start to eat her flesh. I was sickened by the fact that the Lord above would allow such a miserable creature access to our world. What pissed me off, even more, was that the police would never find this girl; the family would never have a body to place at rest. I thought about the most horrific ways to end him. What could I do to make him suffer?

I thought, "Take your own life! Take scissors and cut your leg to the bone. Eat on your own flesh until you bleed out." The man stopped what he was doing and got up to find scissors. He placed the scissors to his leg, and he began to cut until I could see bone. As he cut, he peeled his flesh off and started to eat it.

I stopped him and thought, "Stick the scissors into your heart." The man stopped, turned the scissors toward himself, and thrust as hard as he could into his own heart. I heard him gasp a few times and fall from his chair. I would reveal the real face of fear as he rose from his body. The man wriggled around and finally died. He rose and looked at me.

"Who are you?"

"I was sent here to make sure that you hurt nobody else. I was sent here to make sure you died." I stood there and stared at him. I was waiting for the pit to open, but it did not. Why wasn't this man going to Hell?

"Where are you going to take me?" I wasn't sure how to answer him; this had never happened before. The door of the house opened, and another man walked in with grocery bags. "Shit!" he started yelling. "That little prick got loose and started without me!" It hit me: I had killed the wrong man! This was a sick man who was being tortured by the other man. That had to be the reason that the man I was standing with did not cross. I looked at the man I had just killed.

"Is this what you wanted to do?" I asked him.

"No. Harold told me to drink and eat the little girl to get rid of her body. He went to the store to get things to cook her with. I didn't want to do it, but he said he would kill me if I didn't. I was scared, so I started before he returned."

I felt pain inside my head, and the angel appeared. "Victor, you have dispatched an innocent soul. You have shown no mercy in it, and now you owe me, one soul."

I watched the angel of death walk over and say, "Surprise!" to the other man. The man turned and looked. He screamed as the angel ripped his heart from his chest and fell to the ground. As he rose from his body, the angel grabbed him from his hair. "I now condemn you to Hell!" A pit opened beneath the man, and the angel threw him in. The angel walked over, grabbed the man that I had killed, and threw him in, as well.

"I have no use for a moronic ghost walking around this earth. Victor, you have made a mistake that will cost you dearly. You have let revenge consume you. You failed to provide a function but instead provided judgment. It is not up to us to judge anyone. We kill who we are supposed to, and you killed an innocent person. One that was to live to make a difference and be studied for mental illness, but that won't happen now."

"I am sorry. I didn't know. I made a mistake."

"Similar to the mistake that took your life, Victor? It was not malice that killed your family; it was a wrong address. I do not agree with the fact that your family was taken, but you have just committed the very same act, so to speak." The angel looked at me with those empty eye sockets. "You now owe me a soul. I do not care where it comes from, and I do not care how long it takes. You also will not be allowed to enact your revenge on the man that killed you. This is the soul that I will take in payment for the one you owe me."

"You sent me here on half-truths and bullshit. You knew damn well that I would dispatch that man, and you did nothing to stop it. You said that you are in control of all deaths; that is how I know you lied to me."

"I told you to be careful what you wished for, Victor! I told you that you would be in charge of killing evil people. Who do you really think you are working for? You have made a deal with the devil, Victor, and those deals are not easily broken. Everyone that you kill is another soul for me," He continued. "I have accepted your payment, and I will stand by my end of the bargain. You will stay in my service and continue to kill until the man that killed you dies, and I have his soul in my possession. Then, if God will have you, he can. If he won't, you can either wander the earth or continue the horrible job I have given you. I will spare you the fire and pit of Hell."

"So, you are the devil."

"I am not. I am the one that finds hapless souls, and I talk them into working for the darkness. I answer to him, and you answer to me so, in all reality I suppose, to you I am the devil."

I could not understand why the angel at the drug lords' warehouse had not told me this. Maybe he tried, and I didn't listen. I looked back at the devil's minion, "So I cannot kill the man that killed me, and I am not free until he dies. Right?"

"You are correct, Victor."

I had the information I needed; I would return after the man that killed me was dead.

"Victor, I have another job for you."

"Keep it, I have one of my own," I replied. I walked out of that apartment to look for the man that killed my family.

Chapter 4

Revenge with a Price

I searched for days for the man that had killed us. I finally caught up with him as he was getting ready to throw a body into the Hudson River. Walking close to him, I yelled, "Hey!" The man looked around wildly. "Who said that!? Who is out here messing with me?"

"Remember the family you killed? The ones that lived at the address you screwed up on?"

The man turned white as a sheet, "I killed you, man! I killed you dead!"

"You killed innocent people. I am sure we were not the first, but the body on the ground in front of you will be your last!"

The man jumped into his car and sped off, leaving the body lying there. "Now, the police will find the body, and if I am to spend the rest of his life waiting, I'm OK with it," I thought to myself. I found it easy to follow the man; no matter how fast he drove, he could not lose me.

"Can you feel the hands of revenge tightening around your throat?"

The man let out a scream. "Why are you haunting me?!"

I am not leaving your side until you see my face at the time of your death!"

The man slammed the gas pedal to the floor. "Get away from me!" he screamed.

"No. I am going to stick to you until you take your last breath," I said.

The man drove faster and faster until he lost control of the car and slid under a semi-trailer. The car collapsed like a can being smashed. I stood outside of the car as the man that killed my family struggled to take his last breaths. I turned away as the man's soul rose from the wreckage. I didn't want him to see my face yet.

"Turn and face me, you prick!" the man said. I turned, and he gasped as he stared into my empty eye sockets. I looked into his face. "Welcome to Hell. They'll be here in a second." The pit began to open under the man's feet, and the claw I had seen many times before grabbed the man by the leg. He screamed loudly as the claw tightened around his leg, and he began to catch fire. "Goodbye. I hope eternity keeps you warm," I said. The man disappeared into the puddle of blackness. The angel that had recruited me to this horrible job appeared.

"I told you that his soul would make us even, but you killed him. The deal is nullified."

"I could give a shit less what you do to me now, you freak. Do what you will."

In an instant, my flesh returned to my body. "I will grant you your flesh back so that it may burn in the pit I condemn you to."

"I'm waiting," I responded, smiling. Nothing happened.

"Master! Take him now. He has broken his end of the bargain. He killed the man that took his life," he cried.

I looked into the emptiness of the angel's eye sockets. "I did not take his life. I simply watched as he died in an accident that I had nothing to do with. It was not my doing if he could not handle being haunted by the man he killed."

The angel came to me and grabbed my throat. "There are fates worse than the death you suffered!"

I felt his bony hands tighten around my throat, and my feet come off of the ground, when a voice from behind me said, "Put him down!" The angel dropped me.

"Master, he has betrayed me. He should pay. He went against the contract." I turned to see a man dressed in a black suit; his eyes were completely black.

"You are the one that betrayed the contract. You tricked him into killing an innocent, and then you tried to use this act to seal his soul as yours. All souls in Hell are mine!" With a wave of his hand, the angel started to sink into a black puddle like the ones I had seen others sink into. The angel screamed in pain as he sank, and then he was gone.

I knew in that instant that I was in the presence of the devil himself. He looked at me. "He has served me for 400 years. He brought me every evil soul you can ever think of. I cannot replace him easily."

"I am not sure what you are going to do, but I will take eternal damnation before I take another life in your name."

"I have no intention of damning you or making you take any more lives," he replied with a smile. I do not let souls in my employ make their own rules, that is up to me. I grant your soul back to you, and your contract is fulfilled." I couldn't believe what I heard. I didn't know whether to thank him or run.

"Where will I go?" I asked.

"You will go wherever the Lord of Heaven decides for you to go. I will tell you this; however, you have killed with revenge in your heart. The Lord may not be able to see clear of that. You may end up with me anyway." An angel, more beautiful than I could have ever imagined, appeared, and a brilliant light surrounded him.

"Michael, I did not think you would come here yourself," the black-suited man said to the angel.

"I am only here because you are here, Lucifer. You need to go now. The Lord has granted you this moment here. Leave and do not return again."

The man in black turned to me, "If I do see you again, you will be made to kill again. I need to replace my loss, and you have already proven you are effective. Farewell for now," he said before melting into a black puddle.

"You have been placed in an unfortunate situation. You were taken before your time, and you watched your family taken, as well. Unfortunately, you will only remember them the way you saw them last. The Lord forgives you for what it was that you were tricked into doing, and that is not the reason you will not be allowed into his kingdom. The reason that you will not be allowed in is that you thought of nothing but revenge. The angel of heaven told you this, he even wept for you, and you did not heed his warning."

"I beg for your mercy. I will accept the penance that the Lord has instructed you to give me," I said, falling to my knees before him.

"The Lord instructed me to look for hope. I looked into your heart and found none," he responded, looking deeply into my eyes. "You are happy that the man died in the car. You are happy that, indirectly, you are responsible."

"I am. I cannot deny it," I responded, my eyes downcast.

"That is why I cannot take you with me. I wish I could, but it cannot be. We had hoped that you would not let revenge taint your soul, but it has. If that darkness is allowed into our Father's realm, it will no longer be heaven, and the purity of the soul will leave. You must be sorry and repent for your sins. You have repented, but you are not sorry, and that is why you will stay here."

"Stay here?"

"Yes. You will be the spirit that can be heard by those planning revenge. Revenge is never the answer, and the Father wants you to help those like you before they suffer the same fate. You will be protected from Lucifer and his minions, but you will remain here to perform this task until you truly figure out what it means to chase revenge from your heart. I hope that you do someday," he said, sadly. That was the last time that I spoke with an angel.

I have helped many people change the error of their ways with the gift the angel bestowed upon me. I have a feeling that I will perform this task for a long time to come because, to be honest, I can never feel remorse for knowing that the man that killed my family is burning in Hell. I am the one that chased him there. Even though I have not been damned by the Lord, I have damned myself. I cannot forget the savage act toward my family, and I cannot forget the coldness that the man displayed while taking my son's life in front of me. The last memory of my wife and son were not so bad. They were standing in a light, and I know that they are with our Lord. It does not make it easier, but it does make it tolerable. I will never forget them and the Hell I suffered when I witnessed them die. I will repay my debt to humanity, and I will try to save every soul I can from the same fate as mine.

PART X

The Ghost
of
Stillman's Run

Chapter 1

May 14, 1832

By the evening of May 14th, 1832, I was camped with the militia commanded by Major Isaiah Stillman. Our camp was about half a mile northeast of Old Man's Creek, and we were there to persuade Black Hawk to return across the Mississippi. Many of us just wanted them to leave here so we could return home. I was seventeen years old and had just joined the militia six months earlier; I fiercely missed my family. As dusk fell over the campsite, some of our scouts had reported they observed three Sauk warriors traveling toward our encampment. They rode under a white flag of surrender; however, I've heard that the savages will attack you once your guard is let down. I was unpacking my gear after our long march from Dixon's Ferry when I heard a shot echo across the prairie. They had shot and killed one of the Indians, but the other two had fled and managed to escape. I don't know how it happened, but before I realized it, the entire camp was worked into a frenzy and tearing through the prairie after the escaped Indians.

We were riding north when we encountered a large number of Indians lying in wait. Under the light of the moon, they ambushed the front column of men whose horses were still saddled from our long march. Those very same men had now wheeled their horses around and were in full retreat. As we retreated through the camp, Captain Giles ordered his men to hold the hill just south of the campsite so the others could escape. There were twelve of us, and we were ready to fight those savages to the death.

The Indians approached, and we started to fire on them. Our shots were quickly overcome, and we soon were fighting hand to hand with those warriors. I had just clobbered one of the Indians with the butt end of my rifle when I felt a sharp pain in the side of my head. When I awoke, the Indians were gone, and the moonlight was shining down onto the dead bodies of my fallen friends. I noticed that a patch of hair the size of a dollar was cut off their scalps, and taken as a prize for the warriors. I looked around and yelled out, "Any of you alive?" I heard no response in the dimly lit night.

I am not sure how long our stand lasted, but the remainder of our militia had hot-footed it back to Dixon's Ferry by now. I picked up my rifle and headed north, where I knew the Indians were camped. My task would be simple; I would find their position and map it out. I would then return to Dixon's Ferry and hope that the Regulars would have arrived. By tomorrow evening, we would return to the Indian encampment and repay those savages for killing my friends. I traveled for a few hours in the moonlight, and the morning was finally coming. I could see smoke rising in the distance around the spot where the two rivers meet.

I continued on toward the smoke, and I noticed a Sauk warrior standing in the woods about fifteen yards from me. I could not believe that he hadn't seen me. I raised my rifle, and I fired. The Sauk warrior took off toward the smoke, and I pursued him through the woods. He was not moving very quickly like someone that had just been shot at, he just seemed to move slowly and precisely through the woods. I followed at a safe distance, and I was cautious not to be seen. There were hundreds of Sauk and Fox warriors camping where the rivers met, not thousands like we first thought. I would have to make my way back to Dixon's Ferry to inform Major Stillman that the Indian encampment was much smaller than first thought.

I took notice of five newly dug graves on the outer edge of the Indian camp. I found it difficult to believe that they had only lost five warriors when all of us were firing wildly into the night. I traveled up to a high ridge on the west side of their encampment to count the Indians inside. Excluding women and children, there were only around six hundred actual warriors there at the camp. I was pretty sure my count was accurate, as accurate as I could be anyhow. I would wait on the ridge until nightfall, and then start out for Dixon's Ferry and travel by moonlight. I felt strange, not tired, or hungry. I stopped a second to think about it, and realized I had not eaten since before the battle last night. I found it very strange that I had not eaten or drunk anything at all, and yet I wasn't hungry or thirsty. I waited until night and started out for Dixon's Ferry.

DAN NORVELL

Chapter 2

Hold the Hill

I had made it back to the skirmish site near our camp at Old Man's Creek. The night was clear, and the moon was shining brightly. I moved through swiftly, and I counted the bodies of my fallen friends as I made my way through. I found it odd that there were the same amount of bodies there as the number of men who held the hill. Maybe one of the others had been killed in the battle, and I had not taken notice in the fighting last night. I completed my count for Major Stillman and continued on toward Dixon's Ferry. I knew it was essential to let the Major know that Captain Adams was killed in battle and that the number of Indian warriors was much less than first thought.

I traveled as fast as I could down the big river, and through the wooded areas so it would be easier to remain concealed. I met a group of Army Regulars traveling north toward the encampment at Old Man's Creek. I went toward one of the ranking officers that was walking with his men in formation.

"Captain, I have news of the Injun numbers up north. They are camping where the two rivers meet."

The Captain seemed to pay no attention to me at all and continued on with his band of soldiers. I found it very odd that nobody paid any attention to me at all. I turned and kept heading toward Dixon's Ferry knowing that Major Stillman would listen to what I had to say.

I continued on, and within the day, I had arrived at Dixon's Ferry. I walked through the encampment, and each soldier I tried to talk to ignored me. I knew that the Regulars had a disregard for the militia, but these guys really made a point of it. I tried to find Major Stillman, but he was nowhere to be found. I was getting tired of being treated worse than a Regular Militiaman, so I decided I would just head back home. I did not see any militia at the encampment at Dixon's Ferry, so I figured they had all just passed by and continued on home as well. If the Regulars didn't want my help, then that was fine by me.

I started back toward Old Man's Creek and moved with purpose. I lived not far from the battle site to the east, so it wouldn't take long for me to gather my belongings and return home. After a few hours, I came upon the battle site on the hill to find the group of Regulars I passed burying the dead militia. It seemed fitting for them to be buried here, where we had fought so hard to protect the company's retreat. I didn't even stop as I walked by the Regulars; it's not like any of them would pay attention to me anyhow. I gathered my things and continued toward my cabin. As I passed, I heard one of the soldiers say to his Captain, "Captain Lincoln, we have completed the burial. Would you like to say a few words for the fallen militia?" The Captain indicated that he would, and he started to speak. I stopped to listen to him.

"Gentlemen, I am Captain Abraham Lincoln. I find it difficult to find these young men that served as volunteers for the militia of this great State, in the matter of which we did. I regret that we do not have time to give each one of them the proper burial that they deserve for their services to the State of Illinois. I only hope that the Lord blesses each of them and that someday, a proper burial will be given to them. Thank you for your service to the State of Illinois men, may God have mercy on your souls. Amen."

The soldiers left a makeshift cross with one of the fallen men's hat draped over the top of it. Captain Lincoln told the men to gather up their gear and to continue on north. I started to walk away, but I could not let them march into an ambush. Even though Captain Lincoln's Regulars had Army issued flintlocks, they would still not be able to stand up against six hundred Indian warriors. I turned back, and I walked over to the grave first. "It was an honor to serve with you all," I said as I walked by and caught up to the soldiers moving north. I had to move quickly to tell them that they may be walking into a trap.

I moved through the woods and came to a river when I started to yell, "Captain, you may be walking into an ambush! They are at least six hundred strong where the rivers meet!" Nobody acknowledged me. I stood directly in front of the advancing soldiers, and as they moved closer, they passed right through me without even stopping. I held my ground, and they didn't slow at all. What in the Lord's name was going on here? I loaded my rifle, and I fired a shot into the air, but the soldiers kept moving as if they didn't hear a sound.

I stood there on the riverbank, completely dumbfounded. I turned and looked at my reflection in the river only to find I did not have one. I dropped to my knees, and I placed my face as close to the water as I could. There was no face staring back at me. The reality sunk in at once; I had been killed with my friends on that hill and buried alongside them. I was nothing more than a restless spirit trying to find revenge. I did not know what I could do to stop the movement of those soldiers, but I knew that I would try anything I could so they would not suffer the same fate as my friends, and I did.

DAN NORVELL

Chapter 3

Dixon's Ferry

Captain Lincoln's company traveled roughly one mile north of our graves before they set up camp for the night. I was relieved to know that they would not be walking into an ambush tonight. As the men slept, I kept watch with the five that were not sleeping, and I tried to talk to all of them. I had hoped at least one of them might hear me, but none of them did. I decided to go back to the Indian camp and scare them into moving north. I had to try something, anything. I could not stand idly by and watch the young Captain and his men be slaughtered the way we were.

I ran as fast as I could and covered the six miles that separated the two camps within an hour. I was amazed at how quickly I could move without having to dodge trees or worry about breaking my ankles. I sat on the same ridge as yesterday and watched the Indians. Chief Black Hawk was speaking to his group, and I found it odd that I could understand him clearly. He told his band that he wished the scouts sent to our camp had not been fired upon, and he didn't understand why the militia would fire on riders who were under a flag of surrender. He told his warriors that they would move on Old Man's Creek, finish off any militia there, and then toward Dixon's Ferry. Chief Blackhawk would find a much bigger force at Dixon's Ferry than he first realized. My immediate concern were the 53 men that would die first outside of Old Man's Creek. I

---

had to stop the Indians and convince Captain Lincoln to return to Dixon's Ferry.

As I ran away from the Indian camp, I could hear the Sauk and Fox warriors let out loud war whoops, and I knew that they were ready to attack anything that they encountered. I arrived back at the Captain's camp within an hour. For the first time since the battle, I felt out of energy. I stumbled and placed my hand on the rear of one of the horses ahead of me. The horse lunged forward, and I ran to put my hand on the horse's head. "Whoa, easy boy." The horse settled down instantly. I had always had a way with horses, but this horse could see me. This means that if the horse could see me, I might be able to get one of the soldiers to hear me too.

I started to try to talk to the men that were on watch again. However, it proved to be futile. I decided to find where the Captain was, maybe he could hear me in his sleep. I had to try anything. The night was quickly coming to an end, and these men would be joining me as spirits if I didn't do something. I went to the Captain, knelt down, and whispered in his ear. "Captain Lincoln. Sir, you need to return to Dixon's Ferry. You will run into an ambush if you don't." The Captain tossed and turned around, and I heard him mutter, "Dixon's Ferry." For the first time, someone was hearing me. I kept talking into his ear, "Captain, return to Dixon's Ferry!" I felt utterly exhausted for the first time since I had died. I sat down for a while and watched as one by one, the men began to rise for the morning. I could smell the coffee they were making over their fires and remembered how great it felt to drink coffee first thing in the morning. I sure did wish I could have a cup.

The Captain had finally risen for the day and told the men that they would be returning to Dixon's Ferry. He said to them that he had a feeling the Indian force up north might be a little stronger than they would be able to handle at this particular time. I was relieved to know that no more blood would be spilled near Old Man's Creek on this day. My only problem now was that if the Sauk and Fox did make it to Dixon's Ferry, they still outnumbered the Army force there by 2 to 1. I had to return to the Indian camp and figure out a way to make them turn north, away from Dixon's Ferry. Maybe I could scare the horses, or perhaps I could convince Chief Black Hawk in his sleep to try again for peace. I am not sure he would go for that after our scouts had shot his men under a flag of parley. I had to return to their camp and try, though. If I could now understand their speech as a spirit, maybe he would understand me talking in his ear as well. I didn't know if it would work, but I knew I was going to try.

Chapter 4

Ever Vigilant

I made it back to the Indian camp just as they were getting ready to march toward Dixon's Ferry. I knew that Captain Lincoln and his men would be heading back there by now, and they would at least stand a better chance there than they would have at Old Man's Creek. I tried to talk to some of the warriors, but it proved to be a fruitless effort. They were ready for war. I made my way to where Black Hawk was sitting by his morning fire. I sat down next to him as he looked into the dying flames, and I could tell he was not willing to take these men to war. I knew he wished that a negotiation could have happened instead of the slaughter at Old Man's Creek.

I decided to try and talk to the Chief. " Black Hawk, sir, there has been enough death for now. The forces at Dixon's Ferry will cut your men apart. Move north, live to fight another day." I kept saying this over and over, but he couldn't hear me. I said it one last time and placed my face into the smoke that was coming off of the dwindling fire. The Chief stood up with a complete look of astonishment. I heard him say, "What is this?" He stood there for a moment, and spoke, "Oh, spirit of the dead, I have heard and will heed your warning. We will not fight this day." I was amazed and relieved to know that he would not be moving toward Dixon's Ferry.

The great warrior stood before his band and spoke to them, "I have seen through the smoke of my morning fire, a spirit of the dead. He warned us not to attack the forces on the great river today. We will instead move north and take refuge for a time with the Ho-Chunk Nation that has offered to speak with us. These are my wishes."

I could see that the warriors were disappointed, but they would follow the orders of the great Black Hawk. They moved north later that day.

There were many more battles and many more deaths during Black Hawk's War. I was witness to the battles of Kellogg's Grove and Waddam's Grove, where men fought honorably against the raiding Indians. I once again watched the men under the close supervision of Captain Lincoln bury the soldiers that fell in battle. By August of 1832, Black Hawk's force was finally defeated, and the great warrior became a prisoner of war.

I returned to my cabin and watched and waited for the Lord to show me the way home. I still walk the battle site near Old Man's Creek. A memorial was erected there with gravestones to mark the names of the men that stood and died there. I will never forget the men that died with me that night, and I still wait for the bugle to sound that will signal their return to take me home with them.

PART XI

The Best Day

The Best Day

"Mommy! MOMMY!" Andrew yelled to me as I was finishing getting ready in the bathroom.

"I'll be done in just a minute, Andy!" I answered back. Andrew was running all over the house this morning because he was very excited. It was his birthday, and I was taking him to see his Daddy. He always loved to go and see his Daddy.

"Mommy? How old am I now?"

"You are 5, honey," I told him. "You are getting to be such a big boy, I know Daddy is proud of you," I told our son as we finished packing our things and headed out the door and to the car. He was so excited to see his father that he squirmed around while I secured him in his car seat.

"Mommy? How old are you?"

"I am 33, buddy."

"How old is Daddy?"

"35, buddy."

Daddy is older than you!"

"Yes, he is buddy," I told him as I started the car, and we made our way out onto the road. It would take us about an hour to get there, and I turned on the radio as my mind wandered and thought about the best day I had ever had.

I remembered that Dale and I had been having a very rough time. We were always fighting, and before he left for his road trip, we had decided to file for divorce when he got back. The love was gone. He had become so consumed with making money, he never turned down a long haul. Ever. When he started consistently taking loads across the country on holidays, that is when I decided I had enough. I never thought things would ever be good again, but I look into that little face, and I see Dale, and I know that when he was conceived that it was a miracle. It was our best day.

Dale was on a week-long haul, and I had been packing things away at our house. I expected him back that Saturday night, and we would decide when to meet with the lawyer and get the divorce underway. I ordered a pizza and was watching television early that Friday when I heard the back door in the kitchen open.

"Hello?" I yelled.

"Karen! It's me. I need you to come here, I have something for you."

"Dale, I am not interested in what you have for me," I answered angrily. I was still so mad at him for telling me it was over, I still had nothing to say to him. I think that him yelling for me was the first complete sentence he had spoken to me in weeks since we decided to divorce.

"Karen, don't be that way. Come here, I have something for you."

"Just a second," I answered as I got up from the couch and made my way into the kitchen where he was. I turned the corner in the hallway and entered the kitchen, "What the heck do you want?" I said as I looked in amazement at the dozen roses, he was holding in his hand.

"These are for you. I know I don't have much time until we are separated, but as I was driving and staring at the picture I keep of you in the truck, I knew I needed to do this." Dale told me as he looked deeply into my eyes.

"What are you doing, Dale? I thought that we had decided that this was over. I have tried to discuss things with you, I have tried to make it better. You were the one that wanted this, not me." I told him coldly. "You can keep the roses and get back into your beloved truck."

"Karen, come here." He said as he dropped the dozen beautiful roses to the floor and reached for me. He pulled me close and looked deeply into my eyes. Dale's eyes were the deepest blue eyes I had ever seen, and one of the things that made me instantly attracted to him when we first met.

"Karen, I am sorry for letting work consume me. I know I was wrong, and I came home as fast as I could so I could tell you. I couldn't wait any longer."

"Dale! Let me go. We had our chance, and you blew it. Just go. I just want you to leave me alone," I told him as I felt his grip loosen around my wrist.

"Ok, Karen. If that's what you want, I'll leave. You'll never see me again." He told me as he turned away and started for the door. He looked so beaten and genuinely hurt by my reaction that I could not let him leave.

"Dale... wait," I said to him, "What did you mean that you were wrong?"

"I was wrong for the way I have treated you. You have been hanging on for so many years now, hoping for a miracle. We have always put off everything for my career, a baby, moving south, everything. I just thought... no, I needed to tell you that I still love you," He said quietly. I could hear the sorrow in his voice.

"Dale, Why now? What has kept you from telling me all of this before?" I asked.

"Karen, it's now or never. I don't know how much time we have left. When we got married, and I chose this career, I always thought that we had so much time. Time is the most precious thing to me right now. Time, and you."

"I don't know, Dale," I said as I began to cry. "You have hurt me so badly. Can't we just talk about this tomorrow?"

"What if tomorrow never comes, Karen?"

He said as he grabbed me and pulled me close. "What if all we had left was tonight?"

"Dale, you are scaring me. Are you ok? Are you taking drugs?" I asked him between my tears.

"I am sober, and I am asking you now," He said as he stared right into my eyes, "can we put our petty bickering and fighting behind us tonight? Can we just act like it is our wedding night and forget all of the pain of the last few years? Can we just spend this night as if it was our last night together?"

"Dale, I don't know," I said as I wiped the tears from my face. "So much had happened..." I tried to say as Dale began to kiss me more deeply than he had ever kissed me before. Dale picked me up into his arms and carried me up the stairs and to our bedroom. It was better than our wedding night.

When the morning sunlight started to pierce the darkness of our bedroom, I felt as if all of the suffering and fighting of the past few years no longer mattered. I had my husband back, and he still loved me. As I ran my fingers through his hair, I whispered, "I have never stopped loving you."

"I know." He replied as I felt tears fall onto my chest. "I was foolish, Karen. I was foolish, and I had my world laid right out in front of me.

I had you right in front of me. Money and material things should never have been what was important. It should have only been us. I'm sorry."

"I know you are sorry, Dale. Let's just put it behind us and look forward to the future." I told him.

"Karen, no matter what happens, and where life will ever take us, I want you to know that I have never loved you more than I do right at this moment. I will always be with you. Always," He told me.

"What do you mean by that?" I asked him with concern in my voice.

"You just needed to know that," he said as he popped out of bed.

"Get dressed, I am going to make you breakfast."

"Right now?" I asked, puzzled. "Don't we have time for that later?"

"Yes, Karen. Right now," he answered as I heard him run down the stairs. I could hear pots and pans being pulled out of the cabinets as I went into the bathroom to get myself in order. I could smell the bacon and coffee, drawing me down to the kitchen to continue our best day together.

"Mommy! We are here!" Andrew excitedly yelled as I popped out of my trance of memory. It hadn't even seemed like we had been on the road that long yet.

"Mommy, did you bring the flower for Daddy?"

"I did, sweetheart," I told him as I handed him the rose. His little legs running across the grass holding the rose looked so funny.

"Hi, Daddy!" Andrew said as he placed the rose on Dale's gravestone.

"Mommy and I love you. Mommy, can Daddy hear me?" Andrew asked me.

"I know he can buddy," I told him.

"How do you know, Mommy?" Andrew asked me.

"I know because I believe in miracles. You are a miracle." I told him. Our son smiled at me and shook his head.

"He looks just like you, Dale. He has your big blue eyes." I said softly as I stared at the gravestone.

As I stood there holding our son's hand, I remembered once again back to that morning. The morning of our best day. The morning I came down to breakfast, and Dale was nowhere to be found.

I remember thinking it had all been a dream. I knew it wasn't because of the eggs and bacon that sat waiting for me on a plate with coffee still steaming in the cup beside the plate and the note that Dale had left for me. I remember frantically running around the house, yelling his name and trying to find him. I remember thinking that he was playing a trick on me. I continued to look around the house and shout Dale's name until I heard a knock on the door. I answered the door, and 2 policemen were standing there. They asked if I was married to Dale Scott. They told me Dale had been killed when his truck had run off the road early in the evening the night before.

I hit the floor and began to wail in grief. A few hours later, my mother and friends had arrived to stay with me, and my mother said that the police had left something for me. My mother told me that they had found it in Dale's hand when they pulled the truck off him. It was a picture of me. Dale had always kept a picture of me in his truck. He told me once that it reminded him of the reason he worked so hard all of the time. I reached into the pocket of my robe and pulled out the note that Dale had left for me that morning. It had 2 sentences written on it. One of the sentences is etched onto Dale's gravestone, it says, "I have never loved you more than I do at this moment."

"Mommy?" Andrew asked me, "Why do you call me a miracle?"

I smiled as I answered him, "I call you that because of something your Daddy wrote to me once."

"What did he write to you, Mommy?" Andrew asked me.

"He wrote, Miracles happen Karen... name him, Andrew," I told him.

"We have to get going, buddy."

We got into the car and started driving away from the cemetery, and I whispered as we pulled away from Dale's grave, "I have never loved you more than I do at this moment."

PART XII

The Gates of Hell

Chapter 1

Meeting Mr. Black

As I sat in the truck, I watched as one of my men looked over at me. He was waiting for my nod to take the life of these police officers that happened on our drug deal. I nodded and watched as my associate shot one of the policemen in the face. The man rolled around, screaming in pain until my other associates opened fire. The policemen were riddled with so many bullets, they would have to remove them all with a magnet. We lit their bodies on fire after cutting off their fingers. We would mail the fingers back to the police department that had sent them to bust us. I always showed no mercy when someone tried to mess up my business. It was never personal; I just needed to set an example for anyone else that thought of crossing me.

We continued our reign of terror for months. I had returned home one night to find that a rival dealer had shot and killed my wife and two children. As I held my dying son, I heard a voice behind me, "Juan, you're finished as the boss." I turned around, and the friend I trusted the most was leveling a gun to my face.

"Johnny, my family had nothing to do with our business, why did you kill them?"

He replied, "I killed them without remorse because I've done it before for you." The gun went off, and the bullet ripped through my skull. I laid on the ground, and I heard the gun go off three more times. In an instant, I was standing in the room, and I was watching Johnny walk out of my house. I looked at myself, and my family laying on the floor of my house. "Dear God! What have I done?!?" I saw a man in a white suit escorting my kids and wife into a white light. I started to follow, and I heard my son say, "Bye, Daddy." The light swallowed them up, and they disappeared. I began to yell, "Where are they! Where did they go?"

I heard a voice behind me, "They have been spared and sent to Heaven, Juan. You, on the other hand, will be finding out what it is like to spend eternity in damnation."

I turned to gaze upon a dark figure. His appearance was that of evil. I asked, "Who are you?"

The figure answered, "I have been called many things. You may call me, Mr. Black." I could not believe what was happening. I could not believe that my life had ended the way it had; I didn't even see it coming. The worst part about it was my family had died for my sins. They were innocent.

I asked Mr. Black, "What happens to me now?" His reply was, "Now... you'll be taken to find out what true suffering is. You are responsible for over one thousand deaths, Juan. You'll feel their pain. You'll be made mortal, and you will die one thousand times. You'll die once for each death that you ordered. After that, you'll be condemned to Hell for eternity."

I began to shiver with fear. I never thought of anything but money and revenge in my years as a drug dealer. I never even considered how many lives had been ended because of me.

"You know Juan, if you could find at least one person that would mourn your passing, I might consider letting you roam the Earth for eternity instead of eternal damnation. I have to be honest, I don't think you'll find them." I knew that Mr. Black was right, there were most likely many that would rejoice to hear I died.

Mr. Black said, "Well, Juan, let's begin your penance. I'm going to make sure that you die and suffer the same mortal death that each of your victims did. You'll suffer each and every death from one to one thousand."

I dropped to my knees, and I prayed to God. I screamed out, "Lord! Lord, I am sorry for my sins! Please forgive me!"

Mr. Black began to laugh, "Do you really think that God the Father will listen to a slimy piece of garbage such as you? You have had no remorse for one single thing in your entire life. You really weren't even a good father to your children. What kind of act are you trying to put on Juan? The Lord is a forgiving one, but not to those such as you. You are mine, and now, the payback begins!"

Next thing I knew, I was in the body of a little boy in a small town in Mexico that I recognized. I could see men walking toward me, and they opened fire at the man standing behind me. I was hit in the legs, and the right side of my chest in the crossfire. As I lay there bleeding, I looked up at myself. I was a young man, and I leveled the gun into my own face.

"Sorry, kid, you should have picked somewhere else to play today." The gun went off, and the pain in my head was excruciating. I could hear people coming near my lifeless body as Mr. Black appeared.

He said, "Oh Juan, I'm sorry. I failed to mention that you get to relive the lives of your victims as they are taken. I bet that when your men filet your legs and arms, and let the vultures eat you alive… that will be real pain. Juan, that's one down, and about nine hundred and ninety-nine to go."

I felt remorse now; I felt sorry for shooting that kid. It was the first murder I had ever committed. I could not believe what a cold heart I had, even as a young man. Mr. Black grabbed my tainted soul from the ground, "It's time to move on to your next victim Juan." I knew this was going to be terrible. I knew I was in for a lot of pain because I chopped this man up with a meat cleaver.

Chapter 2

Mercy

I had relived about 300 deaths of the victims I had created in life. I had been stabbed in the throat, crushed under a press machine, and ran through a meat grinder feet first. I thought back to what a cruel and heartless bastard I had been. I thought to myself, "Is this what death is for everyone?" Mr. Black appeared and had the answer to my thoughts, thoughts that he could clearly hear.

"This is not the way it is for everyone, Juan. You were such a cruel and heartless human. There are things that you have done to other people that even made me wonder how evil you were."

"I have changed Black, I have changed. I don't want this anymore. Can't you just take me to Hell?"

"What do you think this is Juan? Where is Hell? Those people that you killed in cold blood, you are experiencing first hand their Hells. Sometimes before Heaven, comes Hell."

"So, there is hope for salvation for me?" I asked.

"No way in Hell!" Mr. Black answered as he chuckled loudly. "Juan, before we waste any more time, it's time for you to experience your next death."

In an instant, I was hanging by my wrists in a refrigerated room. Two of my men, that I recognized, walked into the room. They stripped me naked, and one of the men started to hold a lighter under my foot. I began to twitch and squeal in pain. "Pablo! Pablo stop! It's me, Juan!"

Pablo stopped burning my foot. "Who did you say you were?"

"It's your boss! Juan! Cut me down now!" The other guy that was with Pablo came up and hit me in the mouth with the butt end of his gun. I spat blood all over the floor.

"You ain't, Juan! You are gonna die for not paying Juan! Pablo, start cutting his feet off!"

They cut off my feet, and the pain was horrible. They turned down the temperature in the refrigerated room so that everything would freeze, and they locked the door and walked out. I basically was left hanging there, bleeding out, but the blood in my legs had frozen, and it was excruciating.

Mr. Black walked into the room wearing a fur coat. "Juan, what did you think you were doing? You tried to get Pablo not to kill you. Those are not the rules of the game, Juan. Mr. Black reached up onto my frozen hands and started snapping my fingers off one by one and dropping them onto the ground. "If you ever try to get your men or yourself from killing again, I will make sure that the Hell you suffer after you have completed this, will make you beg to come back and do it my way. It is history Juan, you can't change it. Deal with it, you created it, you profited from it, now you taste it. Not so frickin funny now, is it?"

"I am sorry for what I have done. I beg for mercy. I didn't know of the pain I caused. Please, God. Please show mercy on my tortured soul."

"You want mercy? A cold-blooded murdering piece of trash like you, Juan? You have got to be kidding," scoffed Mr. Black. "There will be no mercy for you, my friend."

"Go back to Hell and let me die in peace, you dark piece of shit!"

"Flattery will get you nowhere, Juan. You will fulfill the contract that has been arranged. Then you will find yourself in Hell. And Juan, I can tell you now, it's worse than this."

"Stick Hell and your Master up your ass you piece of garbage. I won't beg for mercy again from you!"

"That's it!" Mr. Black said as he ripped my heart out. I watched the heart quit beating as I lost consciousness and died. My soul fell out of the lifeless body and hit the ground. Mr. Black grabbed me by the throat, and I could feel my soul burning. I had never felt anything so horrible, so evil. I began to scream. Mr. Black said, "If you ever insult me again, Juan, I will make sure that your damnation will be far worse than what was originally in store for you. I can make you that promise right now."

Mr. Black released me, and I fell to the ground. I was then whisked into the body of an old woman. I was confused. I had never ever killed an old woman, nor had I ever ordered the death of one. I looked around the room, and I started to recognize the surroundings. I felt a sharp pain in my chest. I could feel the pressure and the pain build as I found it more and more difficult to take my next breath. I tried to call out, but I could not. I looked around the room, and as I lay there dying, I knew that I had just felt what my grandmother experienced when she died. I had just been sentenced to five years in prison, and she must have found out, and the strain was too much for her. I knew this because my grandmother had died while I was going to prison. I never got to say goodbye to her. As I was struggling for my last breath, I could feel life slipping away.

Mr. Black appeared again to me. "I know you are wondering why you are feeling your grandmother's death right about now. I told you, Juan, you would experience each death that you were responsible for. That is the ironic Hell you must face."

I knew that Mr. Black had just dealt me a hand I had not bargained for this time. I had just finished feeling my grandmother's death when Mr. Black told me that I only had about 549 deaths left. Mr. Black could feel the anguish in my soul.

"Juan, don't be such a weakling about all of this. If you think this was bad, wait until you experience the abortion that you made your wife have because you thought the child wasn't yours. It was Juan. And then, you had her killed. I'd venture to say that those two deaths will be very taxing on your damned and tortured soul, my friend."

"I'm not your friend," I told him smugly.

"Careful Juan. If I feel insulted again, I'm quite sure you will not like what I have in store for you this time."

If there was anything positive I could say for Mr. Black, it was that his perception was dead on. He was right when he said that suffering the fates of the innocents I killed would be the worst. I never thought that anything could be worse than death. I also never fathomed that Hell could be anything like this. These deaths that I was experiencing were terrible. The pain that I had caused these people was tremendous. I could not believe that I was even capable of such acts. The shame of it all is that I was capable. I never had anything but a loving mother and father for my whole life. They gave me everything they could, and I repay them by being a rich and powerful scumbag. I really did deserve my fate, and that was clear to me now.

Chapter 3

1,000 Deaths

I was hanging from a tree and feeling the noose around my neck choking me harder and harder. The hanging that my men had just performed was not a success. I hung there and choked and struggled to breathe for around 3 minutes. The pain was intense, and my men began to hit me like I was a punching bag while I hung there dying. Things went black, and I fell to the ground. I was now in the body of an old man. I was in a room, and it was very dark. I heard 2 men speaking back and forth, but I could not recognize the voices.

A shot rang out, and I felt pain in my stomach. I was losing blood, and I felt myself being dragged across gravel and being thrown into the trunk of a car. I knew that the stomach shot might take a while to kill the body I was in, and it was horrible pain. The trunk opened up, and two men I had never seen before dragged me out of the car. They left me lying there on the hillside while they drove stakes into the ground. When they finished, they placed me between the stakes and tied one of my limbs to each stake. I blinked my eyes, and I could feel the birds start to land and pluck the flesh from the wound in my stomach. It was excruciating. I could feel every bite, every quick stab as they would rip the flesh away.

One of the men walked over and slit the side of my face open and cut above my eyes. The birds went to my face like it was a feeding frenzy. I knew that this was the father of one of my competitors. I had ordered my men to think of the worst way they could have someone killed to send a message to him that I was in charge of the drug trade around here. I was now living the death of that man.

The last thing I felt was my eyeballs being ripped from their sockets from those hungry vultures as they feasted on this flesh. Mr. Black appeared as my soul was freed from the dead body. He grabbed me by my neck and made me watch as the vultures cleaned that flesh to the absolute bone. Mr. Black looked me in the eyes, "You were one sick and cruel bastard, Juan. Just when I thought I had seen it all, you had something done that was more ruthless than the last."

"I know it. I was a cruel and horrible man. I know now that I deserve everything that you are doing to me. I accept my fate, and I am truly sorry for everything I have done."

"Well, Juan, you only have about 100 more to go. After that, the real Hell begins. I'm looking forward to acquainting you with real pain."

"I do not care anymore, Black. You can't scare me with your threats anymore. I have been a sick and sadistic bag of bile. I deserve to relive this torture."

"Of that, you can be sure Juan. The next death for you will not be pleasant. You are going to be placed into the body of a young girl that your men repeatedly raped and beat to death. I sincerely am sickened by the tactics you chose."

I was whisked into the body of the young girl. I looked out the back window of the car as it sped away from her father and mother screaming, running after us. One of the men punched me across the face, and when I awoke, it was utterly horrible. Everything those men did and everything that I felt made me feel saddened and humiliated that I would condone such things to happen to people under my order.

I felt my chest tighten, and I felt the last breaths eek from the punctured lungs in the body I occupied. The tears streamed down my face as I died the death of this girl. I knew that it was the last and final straw I was able to take. I felt myself rise from the floor, and Mr. Black was standing there staring at me. I looked at him, "Take me to Hell now. Do your absolute worst. I'll accept it gladly. I can't bear to witness my own cruelty and experience these deaths anymore."

"Well, Juan, that isn't how it works." Mr. Black told me with a look of disgust. "Poor Juan, you just can't seem to grasp that you spread so much chaos onto the world. Have you ever overdosed, Juan? The last 100 deaths you will experience are those of the overdose victims that the very drugs you sold ended."

Some of those deaths were the worst yet. I laid for a month on a hospital bed dying, and it was excruciating. It was not always apparent to those watching just how much pain the body was experiencing. On the morning that the body I had occupied for a month finally died, Mr. Black appeared to me. He looked disgusted and did not look happy. "Juan, that was the last death you had caused. Your contract has been fulfilled." Juan turned and looked at a man standing behind him, "Michael, he is yours. I will be ready to accept his soul should you change your mind."

"That is the deal, Black," Michael told him.

"Come with me, Juan," Michael said as he outstretched his hand toward me. His eyes were the most gentle thing I had ever seen, besides my mother's eyes.

"Who are you? Where are we going?" I asked.

"Juan, I am the angel, Michael. It seems that your penance has been paid. You have truly repented for the sin you have committed. I am here to take you to your family to say goodbye. It is the only mercy you will receive from the Father."

"What do you mean? I am seeing my family?"

"Yes, Juan. You have truly repented for your sin. You will not be spending eternity in Hell, after all. You may spend a short time with your family, and then the Lord is sending you back."

"Sending me back? Back where?"

"Back to do it over, Juan. Back to see if this time you can do it the right way. You have learned compassion, Juan. You truly felt sorry for the souls you took. For that, the Father has granted you a second chance. You will have no memory of what your soul has endured during your time spent in Hell, but you will take your new compassion with you, and it is the hope of us all that it will be enough."

"I have a second chance? That's wonderful."

"Be mindful, Juan. If you go back to your old ways, you will have terrible nightmares that will remind you of your fate. It will be cryptic, but it will spark enough memory to keep you on the right path, hopefully."

"Thank you, Michael. I will not stray from the righteous path again."

Michael walked me to the gates of Heaven, and I was able to kiss my children, my wife, and my parents. I told them how sorry I was that the things I allowed to happen had affected them, and shamed my family and tainted my soul. Michael came to me after an hour and told me it was time. I walked away from my family with a feeling of peace, and I looked forward to returning and making amends in the human race. I would not take the gift I had been given lightly. I would make the best of my new life.

I returned to Heaven 85 years later. I had made the right choices this time, and I had given my life to the church and worked with drug abusers as a priest for my entire life. Only on my death bed surrounded by those that treasured me did I realize I had been given a chance to undo the terrible things that had been done to my soul. Michael was there to greet me, and I was thankful to see him again. I did see Mr. Black again on various occasions. I would see him spinning his stories to the wicked, and he would never look my way whenever I would come to take a soul to Heaven. I knew he always thought that someone that had been so evil could not find peace. It was his greatest failure. I actually thought that when he made my soul relive all of the torture I had been responsible for, it was actually one of his greatest achievements. I believe that is what made it worse for him.

PART XIII

Cell 13

DAN NORVELL

Chapter 1

Cellblock 3, Cell 13

All I remember is working nonstop. I can't remember any time spent with my family. My wife, my kids, it all just seems a distant memory to me. Every waking moment I spend is in this prison. The prison is where I work, it also appears to be where I live. It is where I spend and have spent my life for as long as I can remember. I can remember the riot. The long days afterward, I spent trying to recover, trying to understand the meaning of it all. I work and sleep. The funny thing is, I hardly remember anything other than work. I have been a guard at this prison for over twenty years, since I was 22. I do my rounds, I watch over the inmates, and I keep to myself. I hear the whispers from the cell blocks in the middle of the night. Cellblock 3, Cell 13. It terrifies them. The warden doesn't allow us to use it. I have no idea why.

I continue my nightly watch, I do my rounds, I make my checks. I report to the other officers my findings, but they seem to ignore me. I am one of the older ones, I should have been taken to the top and been pushing pencils by now, but it just wasn't me. I was better off on the floor, better off with the inmates, better off to remain a guard and not a politician. I took this job to make a living, not friends. I walk Cellblock 3, and I never pay any attention to Cell 13. "It's empty, why look?" I always think as I pass. It seems to me that the longer I do my rounds, and the longer I stay to

229

myself, the stranger I feel. The inmates don't even seem to acknowledge me being there. I seem to have become a shadow on the walls of the prison.

It was late one night, and I was walking through the corridor of Cellblock 3. I was passing by Cell 13, and I heard a whisper, "Guard. Guard. What is for breakfast in the morning?"

"Not sure. What are you doing in there? Nobody briefed me that 13 was being used. Who are you?"

"I have been here the whole-time man. What are you talking about?" The whisper asked me.

I peered into the darkness of the cell, but there was nobody there. Not anyone in that cell. I was taken back a bit. "Am I going insane? What in the hell is going on here?" I shook my head and continued my rounds. I think I may need a vacation, but the funny thing is, I can't remember the last time I took one. The next night around the same time, I was passing Cell 13. I could hear shuffling back and forth in the cell, and when I peered into the darkness, and there was nobody there.

"I have got to be losing my mind. I could swear someone was shuffling back and forth in there," I thought to myself.

For the next two weeks, the cell remained still. I never heard anything in there, and the strange things that were going on seemed to become just another memory for me. I was doing my rounds one night, and I overheard two of the other guards talking about the riot. .

"How long ago was it, Jim?"

"It has been 7 years. I was new then, I got called in to help bring things back under control," the other guard told him.

"Let's not be talking about the riot gentlemen. Not a good subject in front of these guys," I said.

They both looked towards me, "Let's just drop it, Ted. Too many bad memories." They both walked away, and the cellblock became quiet. I went and sat at the desk for a moment when I heard the door in Cell 13 bang repeatedly. I quickly got up from the desk and hurried down the corridor toward 13. I could hear someone in there kicking the door of the cell. "Calm down in there!" I yelled as I peered into the window. Nobody was in the cell. As quickly as the commotion started, it stopped. I looked all around me, the corridor was empty, and so was Cell 13.

"What in the hell is going on around here?" I wondered.

Chapter 2

Officer Down

Cell 13 would remain calm for a few days, and then the activity would start again as suddenly as it would stop. I would hear whispering or banging in the cell and run down there to find it empty. Cell 13 seemed to call to me at times, and I felt as if I was going mad. I finally decided to speak to the warden about being transferred off of this block. The prison was a huge place, I could be stationed elsewhere and never have to see this area if I was lucky. Late at night, I was doing a round, and I was approaching Cell 13 the kicking and wailing began. I ran to the door and peered in. Nothing. I walked away, shaking my head. I finished my round and was making my way back to my desk. I passed Cell 13, and I heard, "Why am I being ignored? Why won't any of you talk to me?"

"I will talk to you," I said as I approached the cell. "What are you doing in there? Who are you?"

"I have been left here. Left here to die. I have been here the entire time."

"What is your name?" I asked. No answer was returned from the darkness. I walked back to the desk and slumped into the chair. "I must be going crazy," I thought to myself as I sat there. "It may just be time to look into retiring," I continued to think. I would talk with the warden soon. I think that all of these years in this prison must have been getting to me.

Months passed, and I never seemed to make it to that meeting with the warden. I would start and end my shifts, but I felt as if I would never leave the prison. I can't remember the last time I had even talked with my wife. I couldn't remember the last time I had taken my boys to a ballgame. I couldn't remember anything but working and being here at my post. The post with the voices and the kicks on the door that would ring out from Cell 13. The voice in the cell would call to me. It was getting out of hand.

"Please, God. I must be going crazy. Show me the way," I prayed one night after hearing the banging for hours. Every time I would go to the cell door, the banging would stop. It would begin again whenever I would get back to my desk. It was almost as if I was being toyed with. I picked up my keys and threw them down the hallway, "Stop haunting me!" I screamed. Two other guards ran into the cellblock and looked around.

"Didn't you hear that, Mike? It sounded like somebody's keys went flying down the hallway."

"They were mine!" I shouted. "I have had it with this place! All I ever hear is Cell 13! I am at the end of my rope!"

"I heard the keys hit the floor and slid to a stop, Walter. Man, this place creeps me out. I am glad they shut down this block and this part of the prison after the riot. I hear stuff down here all of the time." Mike said.

"Closed down this part of the prison?" I asked, confused. "I have been working this post for years! What are you guys talking about?"

"Mike, Let's go. There isn't anything down here. It must have been a rat."

"Ok, Walter. But I am asking more about that officer that was killed in the riot. I think he is still here."

"Officer killed in the riot?" What in the heck were these two talking about? I was here during the riot, there was no officer killed. "You guys are crazy! There was nobody killed during that riot!" I told them. They walked away as if I was not even there, and I was once again alone. I walked down and retrieved my keys from the floor of the block and placed them on my key ring. "Officer killed in the riot indeed. I am no rookie gentlemen. You aren't going to get me freaked out by some prison ghost story." I thought.

Chapter 3

Joseph

I sat alone in the cellblock, confused. "What were they talking about? I haven't been dreaming, I have been right here," I thought. I continued to stand my post and do my rounds. For the first time in years, I noticed that those men were right. I peered closely into each and every cell on the block. All of them were empty. There was dust in each cell, and the locks were starting to show corrosion. They hadn't been turned in years it appeared. I walked back to my desk and sat down.

When was the last time I had talked to anybody? When was the last time I had handcuffed an inmate for movement, or taken anybody from here at all? I heard footsteps coming down the hallway. It was the two guards that had been here the other night. They were talking as they walked. I started to think that I didn't even recognize them or the other man walking with them. I decided just to let them talk and just remain here and listen. "Mike. I don't know what you are trying to say." The man told him.

"Warden, I am telling you, there is somebody here. We hear stuff from here all of the time. Don't we, Walter?"

"Yes, sir. The other night it sounded like someone had thrown their keys down the corridor, and they skidded to a stop." Walter told the warden.

"Gentlemen, this block has been closed for over thirty years! The riot is a distant memory for most. I can't have you guys telling ghost stories to the new staff. This job is hard enough without the fear of ghosts!" The warden told them.

"Thirty years!" I thought. "The riot was only about eight years ago now! I have been here the whole time, and I was never made aware of any new warden!"

"Well, sir." Mike said, "I have done some research into the riot, and they left that officer to die at the hands of those prisoners. They killed him in Cell 13! I won't jeopardize my job by telling ghost stories, but I am not convinced he isn't still here either!"

"I agree with Mike, sir. I know that officer still roams these hallways. When you are over in the new section that they added on after the riot, you can hear keys jingling, and cell doors being kicked. He is still here!" Walter said.

The warden looked at both of them, "I'll tell you what gentlemen, this is the last I want to hear of this. If you both want to believe in ghosts, that is up to you. I will not have you two creating stories to mess with the new staff. Demolition will begin soon on this block anyhow. Just let it rest, please."

"We understand, sir. We'll drop it." Mike said as the warden walked away. "Like hell, I'll drop it. They let those prisoners murder that guard, Walter. They let them murder him and did nothing about it."

"That's what I heard too, Mike. The warden doesn't want us talking about it because his uncle was the warden here at the time." Walter told Mike.

"I was here, guys. There was no guard killed in the riot. I agree with the warden, it is a ghost story and nothing more," I told them both. But my words fell onto deaf ears. Those men didn't even acknowledge me.

"Mike. Do you know the officer's name?"

"It was Joseph something or other. I need to do more research. The guy that they housed in Cell 13 was a murderer. They dragged that poor man into his cell and beat him to death. A friend of my uncle worked here at the time. He said you could hear the guard kicking the door and screaming."

"That is horrible, Mike. I know he's here."

"I think you are right, Walter. I just wish he could find peace and move on. I'd hate to think he was stuck here. Especially since they are tearing this part down soon." Mike said.

I walked back to my desk and slumped into the chair. I knew now why things didn't make sense, and nobody would talk to me. I was Joseph. I was beaten to death in Cell 13.

Chapter 4

Negligence

Mike and Walter were good men. Mike stayed true to his word, he would walk down to the cellblock late at night, and he would speak to me. "Joseph? Are you here? You need to go to heaven, Joseph," he would say. I walked up and down the corridor at night. I jingled my keys on their ring to let the two men know I was here. I was walking down to Cell 13 one night. The moon was shining into the small window of the cell, and it illuminated the small room. Peering inside, I couldn't remember anything. It was as if nothing happened.

The last thing I remember about the riot was when it began. I was making sure my cells were locked, and the prisoners were all accounted for. It was reported to put riot gear on, and go to the part of the prison that was out of control. As I walked back down the corridor, I felt a pain in the back of my head. Everything went black. The next thing I remember was sitting at my desk. I heard the other guards speak of the riot for weeks, but they never seemed to answer my questions. I placed my face into my hands, "Dear Lord, take me from this place. Bring me home to see my wife. She has to be with you by now." I looked around and was still sitting at the same desk. The same desk I had been keeping vigil at for years. I once again heard a familiar voice.

"Mike. Did you find anything out?"

"I did, Walter. It's disturbing. Joseph was never beaten to death; it seems. He was checking to make sure that his block was locked down and gearing up. He returned to do one last check and count of his post, and he was shot in the back of the head. He was killed by one of our own in the darkness." Mike said.

"You mean the inmates didn't kill him?" Walter asked in disbelief.

"No. That friend of the family I told you about was here that night. It was an accident. The power got cut off, and it was dark. One of the guards thought Joseph was already in the part of the prison where the riot had started. He opened fire when he saw a figure in the corridor."

"So why was it always said that he was beaten to death by the inmates?" Walter asked.

"There was apparently an insurance policy that the prison had that helped them receive money if a guard were killed in the line of duty during an incident. Joseph was killed by accident, but his death was covered up and spun to the prison's advantage." Mike said with a disgusted voice.

"It was a tragedy, and his family will never know the truth. They could have sued the prison for millions for negligence instead of the few thousand they most likely received for a line of duty death." Walter said.

"Yes, Walter. It seems that our employer was the only one that benefited from Joseph's death. That is what sickens me."

"What are you going to do, Mike?"

"I am not sure, Walter. The warden's uncle is no longer alive. He can't stand trial for what he has done. I am thinking of calling a newspaper, though."

"You will lose your job, Mike. You can't do that."

"A man was killed, and his death was covered up for the benefit of this prison, Walter. They sent the man that was housed in Cell 13 and three others to the chair for that murder. I'd say that my job is worth the truth coming out."

"Mike, you can't bring them back. Think about it."

"You're right, I can't. But I can see to it that their souls find peace and justice." Mike said. I was in complete disbelief at what Mike and Walter had just discussed. If everything was true, then I was killed accidentally, and the prison covered it up and let four men die for my death. It was all wrong, but it did not make sense to me as to why I was still here.

DAN NORVELL

Chapter 5

A Death in Cell 13

I was sitting at the desk I had been at for decades when I heard a commotion in the corridor. I walked around the corner as Mike was being led down the hall by Walter and the warden. Mike was in handcuffs. The warden told Mike as he was being led to the corridor in my block, "I told you to leave well enough alone, Mike. You just couldn't do it, could you? I won't let you wreck my family name with your crusade. Those men are dead, you can't bring them back."

"You're a son of a bitch!" Mike said. "What are you going to do? Kill me too?"

"That is exactly what we are going to do." The warden answered.

"I thought you said we were going to scare him," Walter told the warden.

"There has been a change in plans, Walter." The warden replied.

"Mike, I'm sorry. I wouldn't have agreed to anything if I had known that this was the plan."

"This is the way they do things, Walter. Nothing should have been a surprise to you."

"Both of you shut up now!" The warden told them. "Take him to Cell 13 Walter, and place him in it."

"Move, Mike. I am sorry." Walter told Mike.

I followed them down to Cell 13, went inside, and started to look around. Walter shoved Mike into the cell, and he fell to the floor. The warden walked into the cell, screwing a suppressor onto the handgun he had. "Goodbye, Walter." The warden said as I watched Walter fall to the floor on top of Mike. "I am going to shoot you in the head, Mike. Then I am going to place the gun in your hand and make it look like a murder/suicide. The prison will go on, and this ghost business will be laid to rest. Unless you both haunt it."

"You are a rotten bastard!" Mike screamed. "I hope they figure it out."

"This part will be ripped down by next month, Mike. All evidence of what has happened now or back then will be gone in a heap of stone and metal." The warden replied.

I watched as the warden leveled the gun to Mike's face. I lunged forward at him as the gun went off, and the bullet hit the wall beside us. "Who are you? Where did you come from?" the warden asked, terrified.

"I'm Joseph, and I won't allow you to kill an innocent man in my cellblock," I said. The warden backed out of the cell and closed the door, locking Mike and me in. "I'll be right back, Mike," I told him. I passed through the door as if it wasn't even there and began to walk toward the warden. He fired the gun he had at me several times. I just smiled at him, "You can't kill somebody who's already dead."

"It can't be. It can't be!" the warden screamed as I followed him through the doorway to the adjoining corridor. He kept looking back as I kept following him. He ran out onto the wall of the prison that overlooked the recreation yard. I kept walking toward him, and he fired again as he backed up to the edge of the wall. "The truth will die with me," He said as he jumped headfirst into the yard below. All of the inmates in the yard looked up and pointed. I turned and walked away as the guards and inmates ran toward the body of the warden.

I returned to Mike, and I told him, "Mike, thank you. I didn't realize I was gone. There's a bullet hole in the wall outside of the cell where the round went through my head. That should give you the evidence to call into question the events of the riot."

"I am sorry, Joseph. I am sorry you died."

"Don't be Mike. If I hadn't, you wouldn't be able to prove those four men were innocent of my murder. Thank you again," I told him as I removed his cuffs. The whole cell began to fill with a brilliant white light. I heard my wife's voice behind me, calling me into the light. I shook Mike's hand, "Goodbye, Mike. Make sure my story is told."

"I promise it will be Joseph," Mike told me as I disappeared into the light.

"I am sorry it took me so long to come home," I told my wife.

"Somebody had to save that boy so he could tell your story, Joe. We have the rest of eternity now," she said with a smile.

PART XIV

Final Flight

Chapter 1

Anybody Out There?

Being a pilot was the greatest thing that ever happened to me. When the United States joined the war after Pearl Harbor, I knew I wanted to fly fighter planes. My squadron had seen a lot of action, and I had been involved in three dogfights. It's funny the things you remember as you are flying across an open ocean, on your way to what may be your last flight. We finally met with the enemy, and we engaged them. I watched as my buddies were shot to ribbons in their planes, they blew up and fell hundreds of feet into the water below. We took a beating. All I could hear was the roar of my engine and machine-gun fire all around. Bullets pierced through the side of my plane and hit the canopy. I rolled my aircraft to the left, and I heard bullets riddle the bottom as I felt a quick sharp pain in the middle of my head. I felt myself slump forward as everything faded to black. I didn't even have time to think, everything just disappeared into the darkness.

I awoke to the humming of my engine, a clear blue sky, and the calm blue ocean underneath me. I looked all around for the enemy or my squadron, and there was no one to be found. I was the only plane in the wide-open sky. There was an eerie calm as the engine hummed and carried my plane. "Where in the Hell did everyone go?" I wondered. I called for an answer over the radio and got nothing but static. I looked all around to see nothing but the water and the sky, with no land in sight. I patted down my body to feel if there was blood anywhere, but I felt nothing. I continued to fly on in silence, the only sound I heard was the hum of the engine and static on my radio when I would turn it on. I decided to try and raise someone on the radio this time, "Lt. Hutchinson to squadron. Lt. Hutchinson to squadron. Is anybody OUT THERE DAMN IT!?" The only reply would be static. I flew on for hours, continuing to scan the ocean for land. Night fell, and the sky was clear, the Moon illuminated the cockpit of my plane. I found it strange that I had been flying for hours now, and I wasn't hungry, thirsty, or in need of relief. It was just me and this plane. I flew on through the night, listening to the same hum and static.

As morning sunlight broke the horizon, I began to become nervous. I had been in the air now for at least 18 hours. I should have run out of fuel a few hours ago. I frantically scanned the water for any sign of land, I would have taken a small island with a single tree on it at this point. As the hours passed by, the engine continued to hum, and there was no sign of land. I knew that I should have been out of fuel by now, and yet the engine still purred without missing a beat. I tried my radio again, "Sam! John! It's Hutch, guys! It's HUTCH!! WHERE THE HELL IS EVERYONE?" I screamed over and over into the radio for hours. I knew whatever miracle that kept me in the air for hours would eventually run out, and I would be drowning because I couldn't swim very well. This same scenario played day after day for around 5 days. I was still in the air, and I was still lost. I finally decided that I had enough. There was no explanation for the plane that should have been out of fuel days ago would still be flying. I decided to gain altitude until the engine stalled and fall into the sea. As I throttled the plane higher and began my climb, I spoke into the radio for what would be the last time. "To anyone listening, this is Lt. Pete Hutchinson. I am signing off."

"Lt. Hutchinson, Don't do that. We have a lot to talk about." A voice came across clearly.

"Who am I speaking to?" I asked. "I don't have time for these games! My plane is about out of fuel!"

"Lt. Hutchinson, I can assure you, you have all of the time that you could ever want." The voice replied. "Even if you were to dive that plane into the ocean, you would find yourself back in the cockpit and over the water before you could blink your eyes."

"Who are you? Where are you? What are you?" I asked.

"Who I am is not important right now. What and where I am is not understandable to you." The voice answered. "We will talk again soon, Lt." I was once again flying over the ocean, bewildered at what just happened. My only companions were the hum of the engine and the static from the radio.

Chapter 2

Death Watcher

I flew on for days listening to the sound of the engine and static from the radio. The voice had not returned. I felt as if I was finally going to snap. Maybe I was going crazy? I tried to figure out where I was, and it never proved successful. My compass just uselessly spin. I wanted this torment to come to an end finally. I decided to pull the canopy lever, remove the straps that hold me into the cockpit, and turn the plane upside down until I fell into the water. I may survive, and I may not, but I would find my way out of the Hell I was now enduring. I tried to pull the lever to the canopy, and it was frozen. I tried to pull my straps, and they were all locked tight. I reached for my knife to cut the straps, kick a hole in the canopy, and squeeze through it. But I couldn't find the knife in my pocket. I stopped looking for the knife for a second, "what am I doing?" I thought. "I can't kill myself, that's a sin."

"It is a sin, Lt. Hutchinson," the voice boomed over the radio. "A sin that you're not able to commit anyhow."

"A sin I can't commit anyhow?" I asked. "What do you mean by that? Who are you?"

"You can call me, Mr. Black."

"Mr. Black? What kind of name is that?" I asked.

"The only one that you are going to get Lt."

"Fine, Mr. Black. Where are you?"

"I am watching you, Lt. I am closely monitoring your location. Every hour that passes brings you that much closer to where I am," The voice answered.

"And where is that?" I asked.

"The gates of Hell, Lt. Hutchinson."

"What did you just say?" I asked, with a knot in my stomach.

"I simply answered your question, Lt. Soon, your plane will bring you here to me, and I will welcome you with open arms."

"I have done nothing wrong! I have always been a good man; I have been a good husband, a good son, a good brother, and a good Catholic. I don't deserve this. I am not even dead!" I screamed into the radio.

"You died and were shot down four weeks ago, Lt. Hutchinson. I can assure you, you are dead."

"I was shot down?" I asked with my voice quivering.

"You were. You weren't even aware of it, were you? Sometimes death comes so quickly, there isn't time to be aware." Mr. Black answered.

"This is why I am not hungry. This is why I don't sleep. This is why the engine won't stop." I said.

"That is correct, Lt. The better that engine runs, the faster it delivers your soul to me." Mr. Black replied.

"What did I do to deserve being condemned to Hell? I did my duty and only answered the call when my country asked."

"You've killed dozens of innocent victims, Lt. Your dive-bombing over villages. What kind of person does those things? Does it make it less evil if it was in service of your country?" Mr. Black asked me.

"We retaliated because of the slaughter they started. We only joined the war effort to stop their evil." I told him.

"Evil is a point of view, Lt. Hutchinson. To them, you're the evil ones," Mr. Black replied.

"Then I will turn the plane around, Black. I will fly away from Hell's gates!" I told him.

"Turn the plane around Lt. You'll only delay the inevitable. Your soul is in despair, and it will be mine. There is nothing you can do about it," Mr. Black told me.

"I'll take my chances, Black," I said as I turned my plane around and throttled it higher. "I'll spend eternity in this cockpit before I fly this plane to your gates."

"Do as you must, Lt. You will be mine. There is no way around it now," Mr. Black replied. "You need to realize this."

"I won't accept that, Black. I'll rot in this plane before I accept what you're saying," I said as I could hear the engine of the plane begin to sputter. I could hear a voice calling to me, but it wasn't coming from the radio.

"Pete! Pete!" The voice was calling. "Pete, cut your engine!"

I was not sure why, but I cut the engine, and the plane began to fall toward the water. The water was approaching quickly as I grasped onto the cross I wore around my neck, "please God. I would take it all back if I could, I wouldn't hurt anyone. Please do not condemn me for defending my country," I prayed as the plane hit the water. Everything started to go black as I felt the cold water surround me and fill my lungs; until I saw a bright light. I reached for the light, felt a hand grab me, and begin to pull me from the water. As I broke the surface, I recognized the face of the man pulling me out. It was my father. "Dad, help me!"

"Hold on, son, don't let go of my hand!" My dad told me as he pulled me out of the water onto a shoreline. I lifted my head and looked up as my father backed away from me.

"Dad! Dad don't go. Don't leave me!" I said as I stretched my hand towards him.

"It isn't your time, Pete, you have to take care of your family. I have to go now." My father told me.

"Dad, take me with you. Don't leave me!"

"I'm always with you, son. I always will be." My father said as he disappeared into a brilliant white light. I felt my face hit the sand, and I passed out.

Chapter 3

A Last Goodbye

I woke up to my friend Sam holding my hand as they wheeled me into the hospital back at the base. "Hutch! Stay with me, brother!"

"My dad, Sam, where is my dad?" I asked him as I grasped his hand tightly.

"Hutch, they have to do surgery now, you hang in there. I'll be by your side." Sam told me as they placed a mask over my face.

I woke up several days later in the hospital. I learned that my plane had been shot down, and a bullet ripped through my spine. The hardest news was that I was now paralyzed from the waist down. I returned home months later, and as my wife wheeled me to my father's graveside, I looked down at the stone that marked his final resting place. The date on his stone showed that he had died the day before I was shot down. I had spoken to my priest about my ordeal. I told him of Mr. Black, and how it seemed, I was in that cockpit for weeks on end. He told me that maybe it was the devil's way of trying to get me to give up on my life, that it was a complete miracle I had survived at all.

My friend Sam had seen my plane erupt into a fireball as it hit the water, and thought I had died for sure. He told me that it was only a matter of minutes that I could have been in the water before I had washed onto the shoreline. I spent many years questioning the things I had to do in the war, I had even questioned God for letting it happen. I now know that my experience was the Lord's way of telling me not to question my duty to my country. I was sure of one thing; I knew that war was Hell, but the Hell I had endured in the cockpit of my final flight showed me that there was indeed a heaven and that my father was the angel sent to save my soul.

PART XV

For the Love of a Woman

Chapter 1

What Has Changed

I can't believe I just got into an accident, and if that wasn't bad enough, the car was wrecked. Mike was going to be furious. I stood there and watched as the police walked around and marked the scene out. I was in such a hurry to get home, it just happened. It's our anniversary tonight, and I want it to be special even though it'll be overshadowed by the accident. I know Mike will forgive me for the car, I'll just throw myself at him, and we won't talk about anything until tomorrow. Tonight, will be just about us and our marriage.

I made it home, and Mike wasn't here yet. "Good," I thought, that gives me time to get into the gift I got Mike. I put on the lingerie I picked out, skipped dinner, and went right for dessert. I'll make Mike forget all about the car, the accident, his busy day at the office, everything! It seems so strange, but the house feels so empty. It has been dark for hours now, and Mike still isn't home, I'm starting to worry.

There is a key in the door, Mike is back! I rushed to him as he walked into the bedroom. Without a word, I dropped the clothes I was wearing, pushed Mike to the bed, and made love to him for hours. I was determined to make him not even want to think about the car accident and the car being wrecked. I just wanted the night to be special, and I think it was. I was in such a hurry to make

Mike think about me, I didn't even say a word. I know, deep down, Mike knows how much I love him. Our 5th wedding anniversary was a success despite the accident and totaling the car.

It's time to start thinking about children, I thought, as I laid on Mike for the rest of the night. But in the morning, he was gone before I woke up. I'm so tired today, I think I'll just call-in to work. I have never felt so drained of energy. I picked up the phone, and all I heard was static on the line. Come to think of it, when did Mike buy a new phone? And when did Mike switch the living room around? It must have been an anniversary present for me. When Mike gets home, I'm going to tell him I want to start trying to have a baby. I think that I will wear that slinky lingerie I wore last night, that seemed to leave Mike speechless. I think tonight I will make it a repeat of last night. I know Mike really likes it when I just attack him without saying a word.

Nighttime was finally here, and when Mike made it home, I threw him to the bed as I did the night before. As we finished making love, I told him I wanted to have a baby. A soon as I moved off him, Mike got off the bed, put his clothes on, and ran out of the house. What did I say? I thought that my husband would at least talk to me about the fact that I wanted to start a family.

I tried to call Mike at work the next morning when he hadn't returned home. The secretary just kept saying hello, but never answered any of my questions. Is my husband having an affair behind my back? Mike didn't come home for what seemed like a week. I sat there in the dark the night he returned and said, "Mike, look, I think I scared you with what I said, and I'm really sorry. I thought that we both wanted kids. I'm really sorry for putting that on you." Mike didn't say one word. He just blankly stared at me, and turned and walked into the bedroom, and shut off the light. "Fine! I'll sleep on the couch tonight. We need to talk about this, Mike." I got no response from him. He must be having an affair, but wait a minute, this is Mike. This is the man that I love, the man that stood by my side through thick and thin. Mike stood by me and was so supportive when we thought I had cancer, and I know deep down in my soul that Mike would never do anything to hurt me. He must just be busy at work and stressed out about me wanting a baby. It may be best if I don't speak of it anymore, at least until he brings it up.

We spent these last three months living in silence. Mike comes and goes, I try to talk to him, but I just get that same blank stare. He almost looks completely petrified. I try and call him every day, and I never get through to him. Tonight, I'll wear that lingerie I wore that night on our anniversary. I'll just try and make love to my husband, and make him remember why he loves me, and why we need to talk. I am becoming desperate for his affection. Tonight, it'll be perfect. I won't take no for an answer, my marriage is on the line here.

When I heard Mike come through the front door, I jumped into the bed, and when he came in, I would make my move. When he laid down in the bed, I rolled over on top of him. I ripped off his clothes, kissed him, and told him how much I loved him. I made love to Mike for hours that night. I couldn't believe how worn out it was making me. The moonlight was shining in on us, and the moment seemed perfect.

"I miss talking, honey. I miss our marriage, please come back to me. If you want to wait, we can. I'm still young enough to wait a couple of years for kids." Mike just laid on the bed underneath me and said nothing. I grabbed Mike by the face, "are you hearing a word I am saying? Well, that is fine, Mike. If this is what our marriage has become, and sex is all that's keeping us together, fine. We will play it your way! I'm 30 years old, and I'm attractive, and I will fulfill my needs, whether you talk to me or not."

I let go of Mike's face, and in the moonlight, I noticed I had scratched his cheek.

"Mike, I'm sorry." I got off him, and once again, Mike ran from the house. I sat on our bed and cried. I couldn't believe my husband no longer loved me. If sex was all that kept us together, then I would have sex with Mike every chance I got. I would prove to my husband that he was all that was important to me. I had to, he wasn't the same Mike, and all I have to hold onto right now was the intimacy in our bed. That would have to be what sustained me for now, because it was all I have at this point.

Chapter 2

A Woman Scorned

Mike remained distant for weeks, and the more I made love to him, the further the distance became. There were nights that Mike didn't even come home from the office. Our 5th anniversary was supposed to mark a milestone in our marriage. Yet, it seems to have been the very day that everything changed. I feel so depressed and angry, I wonder if things will ever get better? I lay around all day and think of nothing but my husband. I can't even remember the last time we had eaten a meal together or the last time I had eaten a meal at all for that matter. As time went on, every time that Mike would come home, I would throw him to the bed, and I would have sex with him. Sometimes it would be all night, and sometimes I would be gentle. Other times, I would just be there for me, and I really had no concern for my husband, other than I needed him as a partner. I was getting sick and tired of living in silence, and sex was the only thing that I had to hold on to. I needed to get my head on straight. I decided it was time for a night out with the ladies. I hadn't spoken to any of them in so long, and it was time for me to be me for a night.

I called everyone I knew, and never got an answer from any of them. The only one that picked up the phone was Janey, and she just kept saying hello. Well, if nobody wants to go with me, I will go by myself. I looked all over the house for my clothes, but I couldn't find any of them. The only thing I could find was the lingerie and the clothes I wore on the day of the car accident, the day of our anniversary. It was almost a year ago now. A whole year with my husband, and not a single word from his mouth. "Hell with it, tonight is about me. I'll go out by myself, find my appetite, then I will come home, and Mike will be my outlet." I washed my clothes and went out the door.

I looked around the driveway and didn't see my car anywhere. I walked about eleven blocks before I found a bar that looked a bit like the ones I went to with my girlfriends before Mike and I met. I followed a couple of men into the bar, found a corner, and just sat there. I watched people come in and out of the bar, but I never had a drink. I just sat back in a dark corner and wondered where I made my mistake. What was I doing now? This is no way for me to get my marriage back on track. I got up and walked out the door toward home. The house was dark, and the moon was shining brightly. I walked inside and up to our bedroom. I got undressed, stood in the moonlight, and looked at Mike as he laid in bed, sound asleep. I felt so bad that things had gone so wrong. I should've never gone out tonight without letting him know where I was; those games are left to women that cannot grow up.

I laid down beside my husband and put my hand on his back. "Mike? Mike, I am sorry that things ended up this way. I love you." My husband just continued to lay there, with no reply. I began to pull Mike over on top of me, and he woke up startled.

"Mike! It's me, your wife! What in the hell is wrong with you?" I pushed Mike over on his back and got on top of him.

I started to make love to him, and I heard him say, "stop, please stop. I don't know what you want from me, but I really need you to stop."

I looked down at Mike, "What?" I smacked him across the face and got off him. He jumped out of bed, and his eyes scanned the room wildly.

I stepped into the moonlight shining through the window, and Mike said, "I can see you there, and I really want you to leave."

I ran across the room and pushed Mike back onto the bed. I held his hands down tightly, and I started to have sex with him again. "This is all I have left, Michael! You will not deprive me of the only thing that keeps me close to you." I started to feel Mike wiggle around underneath me, and I could hear him groaning.

I began to really get into it when I heard Mike yell, "Stop! Stop and leave me alone, you bitch!"

I stopped and looked down at Mike. "Bitch? In almost six years of marriage, you have never called me a bitch." Mike tried to sit up, and I reached behind him and dug my nails into his back. "I will teach you to call me names." I could feel Mike submit to me, and I jumped off him.

"You can screw yourself, Michael! If this is what you want, then I will leave you alone! I want a divorce." I ran into the kitchen and started throwing things around the house. I broke glasses and plates on the floor. I was out of control. Mike walked into the kitchen and turned the light on, and I walked over to him, and I punched him as hard as I could in the nose. Mike's nose started to bleed as he grabbed his face.

"You will never talk to me like that ever again. I have done nothing but try to be a good wife to you, and I get repaid with you calling me a bitch."

Mike hit the floor, and was on his knees, "Please, just go away! I can't live like this anymore."

I looked at him down on his knees, "Is that what you want, MICHAEL?!"

Mike looked up as the blood streamed from his nose, "who's Michael?"

DAN NORVELL

Chapter 3

Emma

As Mike kneeled on the floor, blood spewing from his nose, I looked at him and said, "what do you mean, who's Michael? You're Michael! You are my husband."

Mike just sat there, and he started to cry out, "Just leave me alone! Go Away! I don't know anyone named Michael."

I staggered back and took a long hard look at the man on the kitchen floor at my house. He looked like Mike, but the harder I looked, the more I realized it wasn't Mike.

"My God, who are you? Where is my husband." The man didn't hear me.

I grabbed my clothes and ran out of the house. Who was this man in my home? Where is Mike? I needed some answers. I went to Janey's house, and I knocked on the door. An older looking woman answered the door and looked around. It looked like Janey, but she was older, much older. I stood there, and the woman didn't even see me when I was right in front of her. The door closed, and I was alone on the porch. I walked down onto the sidewalk and started back to my house. It was the only place that was slightly familiar even though Mike wasn't there.

I entered the house, and it was empty. It was still a mess with the glasses and plates busted on the floor. I went to try and pick the broken dishes up, and I could not. It took me every bit of energy I had to even make a shattered piece of plate move across the floor. I went and laid down on the bed and fell asleep. When I awoke, I could hear a woman's voice. She was calling out to me, but I just ignored her. I had nothing to say. I was confused, and I longed to find out where my husband went. I just sat there on the floor in the bedroom with nothing to say.

I wandered the house for months without crossing paths with the man that now stayed in my house. I am sure whatever I was, I must have scared the hell out of him with my outburst. The man would come home, eat, and sleep on the living room couch with all of the lights on. I had a roommate, but I was alone. I felt terrible that I had been basically raping this man for the past year, thinking he was Mike. What the heck was I? Am I dead? Am I a ghost? I went into the living room where the man was asleep. "I'm so sorry, I'm leaving now," I whispered in his ear. I didn't know where I was going, but I knew somehow it wouldn't be any worse than the Hell I was creating for this man. I walked out of the door of my house for the last time, and I never even turned around to look back at it.

I wandered the streets of the city and found my way back to where the accident had occurred. The street looked very different, as well as the cars that were going up and down it. I walked up to one of the streetlights, and there was a bow tied around it. It said, "In Memory of my Wife." It was tattered and old like it had been there for years. I just stood there, on the street for hours. People walked up and down the sidewalk, cars drove by, and nobody ever took notice of my presence. I walked to the church that Mike and I were married at. If I died in the accident, then Mike would have buried in this church's graveyard.

I had nothing but time now, so I walked through the cemetery and checked each grave, stone by stone, until I finally found mine. I had been killed in the accident, and Mike had bought a beautiful stone in my memory. My death must have dealt quite a blow to Mike, especially on our anniversary. I just wanted to be near him, but I had no idea how to find him, or where he now was. I now know I'm dead, but I need to figure out how long I've been gone. I looked around and found the date on a paper in a newspaper stand. I didn't even take notice of anything but the 2011. The year was 2011, and I had died in 1985. I have been dead for 26 years, and it seems like only a little over a year had passed. It seemed that time didn't apply to me anymore. I decided I would go to Mike's work, wait for him there, and follow him home. Mike would be 58 years old now, and I know I'll recognize him when I see him again.

I went to the building Mike worked at, and the name of the firm was no longer on the building. I struck out. I went back to the cemetery where my remains were and sat beside my grave. I was sitting there when I noticed a gravestone next to mine, with the same name. The birth dates and death dates were 1995 to 2007. The words on the bottom of the stone read, "You made the sunshine in our lives. In memory of our little Emm". Emma was my name, and it seems that Mike was not exempt from further heartache, even after I was taken from him. He lost his little girl too.

Mike and his wife had named their little girl after me, his first wife, the most significant way he could have ever kept my memory alive, in the name he gave his little girl. I decided to sit and wait at the gravesites until Mike came to visit. It turned out that the wait would be a long one. I sat there for several days it seemed, and then one afternoon, a man walked up to the graves with two girls and a woman. They placed flowers on my grave, and on little Emma's. I knew right away that I was looking at the aged face of Mike. He was heavier, and he was gray, but he was Mike.

He knelt at the graves for a while, and his wife put her hand on his shoulder, "Mike, it's time to go. It'll be raining soon."

Mike answered, "I know, I have had many happy years with you, Mary. I regret nothing, but I just want to stay a bit longer with them." Mary agreed, and she told Mike she and their girls would wait in the car for him. Mike sat at the graves, and he started to cry.

I put my hand on his, "Mike, I am so sorry. I wish things hadn't happened this way."

"Emma, she was beautiful. She was the most beautiful little girl. It was fitting that we named her after you." I felt terrible. I watched as Mike got up, and he kissed his hand, and he touched both gravestones. "I Love you both. Keep watching over my little one, Emma." Mike walked off into the dusk, and I was alone in the cemetery once more. I felt so sorry for Mike and Mary. I wondered what had happened to their little girl. I would gladly watch over little Emma if I had known. I was too busy making life hell for another man, and not even thinking about anyone but myself. I turned around to see a little girl standing behind me.

"I died of cancer," she said.

"Emma?" I asked the little girl.

"Yes," she answered. "My Daddy said you would take care of me, and I always waited because I knew you would come."

I looked into those beautiful little eyes, "Your Daddy was right, Emma. I will watch over you, and I promise to never leave your side."

The little girl came up and threw her arms around me, "I haven't talked to anyone in so long, I thought you would never come." I hugged her back, "I' m here now, Emma, I'm here now." I only had one problem, how would I find peace for Emma and me if I didn't know where to look.

Chapter 4

Voices in the Dark

Little Emma's the prettiest little girl I had ever laid eyes on, she's absolutely beautiful. I asked her, "Emma, how long were you sick, sweetie?" Emma told me she had been sick for two years.

"I finally died one night while Daddy was holding my hand. He told me that you would watch over me in heaven. Is this heaven now?" I looked at Emma, "I don't think so, Emma. I believe we're stuck here in the world to help ease your Daddy's pain. Do you remember where you lived, Emma?"

Emma looked at me with those beautiful eyes, "I go there all the time to be with Daddy and Mommy, and my little sisters. They don't see or hear me, but at least I can be with them." Emma took me to Mike and Mary's house, it was beautiful. Emma's sisters were not so little anymore. I don't think Emma sees them as anything but her little sisters, much the way I saw the man in our house as Mike. Emma took me to her room, and Mike and Mary kept it the same as the day she died. Emma looked up at me, "I sleep in my bed every night. I go and kiss Mommy and Daddy every night, and I go to bed by 8:30. That was always my bedtime before I got sick."

I looked at Emma, "tonight, little one, I'll sleep with you in your bed, like a sleepover!" Emma looked at me, excited, "I never got to have any of those. Thank you so much!"

I laid and held little Emma in my arms until we both fell asleep. I found it odd that ghosts got tired and slept. I woke up in the middle of the night, and Emma was gone. I looked all over the house and found her lying at the foot of her mother and father's bed. I picked her up and brought her back into her room with me.

She woke up as I carried her back to her room, "I wanna stay with my Mommy and Daddy."

I looked at her, "I know you do, I wanted to stay with your Daddy after I was gone too. Emma, why did you leave the bedroom?"

"I get scared at night. I get scared of the voice calling to me. It keeps asking me to come with it. It always asks me to be mean to my family."

I looked at her and was concerned. "When do you hear this voice, Emma?"

"I hear the voice every time I'm sleeping, it comes from my closet. That's why I always go and lay by my Mommy and Daddy. I know that they can't help me, but just if I'm with them, it helps."

I looked at Emma, "I won't let anything get you, Emma, I'm here now. I'll keep you close, always." I would later find out that I had to be stronger than I ever had in life. The voice in the closet, it turned out to be something that was after more than just the need to scare the ghost of a little girl. It was after her soul.

Chapter 5

Battle with Darkness

Little Emma and I stayed at the house with her family. Mike became more and more depressed, and finally, one day, Emma and I heard Mike's wife yell at him, "I can't handle it anymore Mike, I lost my little girl too."

Emma ran to me and hugged me. "I hate to see my Mommy and Daddy fight. It's never been this bad."

Emma's sisters were out of the house, and Mike's wife finally said, "I'm leaving Mike; I'm done. I cannot take the lonely feeling I have anymore." With that, she walked out the door.

Emma held me and cried, "It's my fault," she said.

"No, it isn't Emma. You had cancer; you couldn't help it. You stay positive."

For weeks, Mike continued to deteriorate. He became thin, and the presence in Emma's closet grew. It made itself known one night to Emma and me as it went past us and into Mike's bedroom. When I looked into the room, I saw a cloaked figure with no face hovering over Mike's bed, watching him sleep. I told Emma that we would start sleeping in her Daddy's bedroom from here on out. I was walking around Mike's room late one night, and I heard a laugh from Emma's room. I hadn't heard the cloaked figure make noise before, but maybe this was my chance. I checked on Emma, and she was with Mike, sleeping at his feet of his bed. I got up the courage and walked into Emma's room. It was standing in the middle of the room with its back toward me when it finally spoke.

"I am here for the little girl; I am also here for her father."

"Who are you?"

It turned and looked at me, with only two glowing red eyes peering from the darkness of its face. "Who do you think I am?"

I looked in its face and trembled, "You're death."

It started to laugh, "I am worse than death, my dear. I'm Scratch's soul stealer. I'm death for souls after the body dies, and Emma's been on my list for a while now. It won't be hard to take her once her father's dead. Then, I'll have them both."

I was instantly mad, "You won't have Mike or Emma, you son of a bitch! Stay away from my family."

I lunged at it, and until now, I wasn't aware that ghosts could feel pain. But it grabbed my throat, and I felt a terrible burning.

"You don't know what you are dealing with. You were on the verge of me owning you. You were attacking and raping that man. You thought it was your husband, but you were such a selfish bitch. You didn't think for once to leave him alone. You pleasured yourself and thought of only you. You would have been my greatest creation."

He threw me against the wall, and all I could do was I lay there as it looked at me. "Go back to Hell!" I screamed. I heard something behind me; when I looked up, I saw Emma. She was screaming.

"Emmy! EMMY! Daddy's got a gun!"

It gleefully proclaimed, "This is it! This is the day I get two for the price of one! My master will be proud." I felt a strange flutter in the pit of my stomach as I jumped up and pushed it down the steps.

I rushed to Emma, "Sweetie! Come here to Emmy." As I rounded the corner, I heard the shot. Mike's body hit the floor, and blood streamed out of a hole in the side of his head.

Emma screamed, "Daddy! Daddy, NO!" I saw a skeletal hand grab Emma by the ankle and pull her toward it.

It was then that I heard his voice, "Emmy? Emmy, what are you doing here?"

I turned, "Mike! Mike, get Emma away from it. Get Emma away from it and run as far as you can. I'll hold it here."

I realized in an instant that Mike was dead and was now in the realm that Emma and I occupied. Mike ran toward it and grabbed little Emma.

"Daddy! Daddy, you can see me! Help me, Daddy!" Mike went up to it and punched it as hard as I have ever seen a punch being thrown.

"I will not fail my daughter again." Mike somehow got Emma from it and ran toward me with Emma in his arms.

"Mike! Mike, go to the light, Mike! Go and take Emma through the light! He wants your souls."

Mike looked at me, "Emmy. Emmy come with us. I can't lose you again."

"Mike, Emma is me. She represents me. She needs you on the other side with her. Go, Mike, he's death to the dead, and he's getting stronger. Go!"

"I won't leave you, Emmy."

I turned and looked at Mike, "Mike! We don't have time! I Love you. I Love you both! Go, Mike. The light is at the end of the hallway! It won't stay long."

Emma was screaming, "Emmy! EMMY! I Love You."

I heard it coming up the stairway, as it rounded the corner, I concentrated on everything I had. Its head was on fire. It tried to push past me, but I grabbed it's cloak. I pulled myself onto it and wrapped my arms around its neck, and my legs around its torso.

Mike turned before entering the light, "Emmy! Emmy, you take her. Let it take me." I looked up at Mike, this thing was gaining ground toward him, and my energy was depleting fast.

"Mike! Mike, Go."

I looked up and saw an angel walk through the light. It grabbed Mike and Emma, and they disappeared through the light and disappeared. The thing slung me across the hallway and into the bedroom.

"I will take your soul now, bitch."

"I know you will, I sacrificed myself for my husband and daughter."

The last thing I saw as a ghost of a human was a skeletal hand rip into my head. I finally felt the pain of death. As the light of my soul turned dark, I could feel nothing but emptiness and contempt. I felt hatred for the entire human race.

That thing looked at me, "You haven't even felt pain yet bitch, your soul is now mine. There are worse things than death."

It dragged me through the house and out the door by my face. I felt paralyzed for hours, my body was on fire, and the pain was terrible. It finally stopped at an old well out in the middle of nowhere.

"This is my gateway to Hell. I'll enjoy it when the master places your flesh back onto your body and lets me burn it back off. I love that smell! You cost me two souls, so I'll torture yours twice as hard."

I heard a rumbling underneath of us, and a dark hole started to open. I thought to myself, "I won't regret saving the man I love and our child." She wasn't mine, but I cared for her since that day in the cemetery. I was as close to a mother as she could get since her death. I couldn't have loved that little girl any more than if she were mine. I felt it shove its hand through my chest, and I let out a gasp.

"Time to go to Hell, Bitch."

We started down the hole, and everything went black. I heard it laugh as we began our trip downward. Right before the hole closed completely, I heard Emma. "Emmy!"

I opened my eyes to the most beautiful place I had ever seen. Mike was standing there with Emma. He hugged me.

"I have missed you ever since you were taken from me. I have missed you both so much."

I looked at Mike, "What happened? I was on my way to Hell."

Mike looked at me, "Saint Michael thought differently. That demon will never take another soul. I heard it tell you there are fates worse than death, Saint Michael made sure it experiences that firsthand." I was saved. My soul was saved by Saint Michael because I was willing to give up my soul for the souls of others. For the first time in decades, I was glad to be at peace with my loved ones.

PART XVI

Double Jack

Chapter 1

The Animal That is You

He had always been there since I was 13. The only time I see him is after he does something terrible. I see him in the mirror, mocking me, making me feel horrible for the crimes he has committed. I should have done something about it when I was younger; when he killed and mutilated my best friend in the world. I loved that dog. My mother and father took me to doctors, they tried to find explanations, they all talked, they all said he was somebody I must have made up. I made him up to cope with feeling helpless during the divorce of my parents. With time and therapy, I believed them; I thought he was gone. I thought that he was erased from my mind. I managed to get on with my life, I have a career, a house, a car, a girlfriend. I thought I was on my way to promotions, marriage, and the perfect life. I hadn't seen or heard him for over 18 years. 18 years of being suppression and silence. 18 years of him plotting his escape. After 18 years, he found his way out of the blocks I set up in my mind to trap him. I found out in one night, some things get very pissed off when they've been trapped for so long.

"Detective! Where's the case file on that murdered girl? I've given you and Colby more than enough time to wrap this up."

"It's coming, Captain. We just have a few more things to tie up, and you'll have it."

"I'd better have it on my desk before the end of shift tomorrow night, or I'll have both of your asses! Understand me, Jack?"

"You'll have it, sir," I answered him. This murdered girl case seemed so vivid to me. Colby and I were assigned this case a week ago, and there were still no leads to who might have killed and mutilated this poor girl. I always approached my cases by trying to understand that sometimes people are placed into situations that they cannot get out of. Many of the other detectives just thought of them as hookers and streetwalkers. I tried to maintain that even though they may have made some unpleasant choices in their lives, they were still people. I guess it is my Catholic upbringing.

"Hey, Colby. The Captain is pretty hot about this one. We need to go over this thing again. We must have missed something."

"We didn't miss anything, Jack," my partner replied as she sipped on a fresh cup of coffee. "The reports are there from the Medical Examiner, and it's just as fricken disturbing now as it was then. This girl was still alive when this animal started carving her up."

"Colby, I know how horrible it was. I read the report. Are you ok?"

"No, Jack. I'm not ok. There is nothing. No evidence. Nothing besides a body, or what's left of it. Whoever is doing this, he does it with the precision of a surgeon. The M.E. said she couldn't have performed better cuts herself. This guy is smart Jack, smart enough to know police investigators, smart enough to be a doctor, smart enough to cover his tracks. It just pisses me off."

"I know, Colby. I know we're doing our best, but the Captain is ready to rip us both new asses if we don't find something. There has to be something. Something we missed."

"We didn't. Trust me," Colby answered.

"Why don't you go home and get some sleep. We'll pick it up tomorrow," I told her.

"Alright, Jack. Goodnight."

"Goodnight," I told her as I grabbed my keys off of my desk. I drove past the crime scene on my way home. I watched as the other girls that worked these streets stared daggers into my soul. I stopped the car, got out, and walked over to where the body was found. "This is no way for anybody to die."

"Yes, it is."

I spun around, startled, "Who said that?" I asked as I scanned the alleyway. "Who's there?" I asked again as I reached for my gun. Nobody answered. I walked out of the alley and spoke to a couple of the girls working there. I asked questions, but they weren't responding. I told them to be careful and got back into my car. I started to drive, and I heard a whisper from behind me.

"She got what she deserved."

"Who's there!" I yelled as I slammed on the brakes. I quickly turned around to look into an empty back seat; there was nobody there. I shook my head and slowly started back down the road. When I finally arrived at my house, I began to think that maybe the case is just weighing on me. Perhaps I was just stressed out too much. I walked into the house and threw the keys on the table.

"Hi Jack," I heard as I turned around to see my girlfriend inviting me towards the bedroom. After she had fallen asleep, I was drifting in and out watching TV as my thoughts raced about the slain girl. I awoke suddenly to find that I was standing over my girlfriend and holding a surgical scalpel in my right hand. My girlfriend was asleep, and I was holding the scalpel about three inches from her stomach.

"What the Hell?" I gasped as I dropped the scalpel on the floor. I turned and ran into the bathroom and shut the door. I started to splash cold water into my face as I heard a voice, that I hadn't heard in over 18 years, from the mirror in front of me.

"Aren't you going to welcome me home, Jack?"

"What the Hell?" I asked, as I stared into the mirror at a reflection of myself that looked back at me with cold and dark evil in its eyes. "You aren't real, I put you away, I blocked you out, I made you! You are nothing!"

"I am you, Jack. I am the animal that is you! You only thought you got rid of me, but you don't know yourself very well, do you? Remember that dream you had 3 days ago about killing and cutting up that whore? Does somebody on a slab look familiar to you? Isn't it ironic that you would be assigned to work the case that you perpetrated?"

"Screw You!" I screamed as I punched the mirror, and it shattered, cutting my right hand to ribbons. I heard my girlfriend pounding on the bathroom door as blood ran down my arm.

"You're still a pussy, Jack." I heard him whisper as he laughed at me.

Chapter 2

Mirror Image

"Come on, Colby, pick up." I thought as I was calling my partner.

"Hello?"

"Hey, Partner. I won't be in today. I had a little accident last night."

"What happened, Jack?"

"I slipped in the bathroom and put my hand through the mirror. I have about 25 stitches in my right hand, and I'm pretty sore right now."

"Ok, Jack. Does the Captain know?"

"Yeah, I called him from the hospital last night. I'll see you tomorrow Colby."

"Ok, Jack. I'll see you then," she replied as I heard the phone disconnect. I paced back and forth in my house, wondering why this thing from my past resurfaced now to screw up my life. I thought about what it had told me, about my dream I had about the dead girl, about how she was my victim. I was in bed that night, I never left the house, Andrea would have asked me where I had gone that night. There is no possible way that I could have killed that girl. I do remember the dream, and the girl in the dream does resemble the victim a little, but there is no way I could have done this.

"Careful, Jack. I know your thoughts," I heard it whisper.

"Who the Hell are you? Why do you have to screw with me?"

"I told you, Jack, I am you. You are screwing up your own life, I am just laughing about it. You are fulfilling the function that your God intended for you. You aren't a good person Jack, you are an animal, a predator, a killer."

"You are a lying son of a bitch!"

"Jack, Jack! Is that any way to talk to yourself? You are so hostile. It's a wonder that people didn't die around you sooner. If you would just accept the fact that you are a sick bastard, this would be much easier for both of us."

"What would be much easier?" I asked.

"It would be much easier for me to take over and run things for us. I've been caged long enough. It's time to spread my wings; continue my work."

"You take over? You are just a voice in my head, a reflection in my mirror, you aren't even real!"

"I'm not? Let me ask you this, was it you or me that was going to carve into your sweet Andrea last night?"

"Stay away from her, you piece of shit! Stay away from her, or I'll…"

"You'll do what? I am there every time you are with her. I watch her sleep when you do, I feel her kiss when you do, the only difference between us is that you love her, and I'd love to kill her."

"You stay away from her. I don't know what you want or why you came back, but you can leave anytime. You have worn out your welcome here," I scolded him.

"You can't make a part of you leave, Jack. It's a fact that human nature eventually becomes self-serving. You can't continue to deny your nature."

"What is my nature?" I asked him.

"To kill," he answered. "First, Jack, I'll make you kill that sweet little partner of yours. Then I'll make you kill more of those filthy whores," he told me gleefully.

"I won't. I won't kill anybody, and you leave Colby out of this," I warned him.

"Jack, I am not doing this, you are. Can I ask you a question? Why are you arguing with yourself anyway? You've suppressed this part of you for 18 years, don't you think it's time to stretch those legs?" he taunted.

"I'm not listening anymore. Leave me alone. I have work to do," I told him as I sat at my kitchen table with my case file. I thought if I submerged myself into my work that he would leave me alone. I sat there looking through the file for what seemed to be just minutes but had actually been hours. He hadn't said a word in that time. Andrea walked through the door and looked at my case file on the table.

"Bringing work home again? You're supposed to be resting. The doctor told you to take a week off and heal," she said.

"I am looking over the file on a murder investigation that Colby and I are working on. We seem to be missing something here. We don't know what it is," I told her.

"Well, good luck. I am going to stay at my Mother's house tonight. I have to be in early tomorrow since I was late today. She lives so much closer; I can get a bit more sleep that way. I just stopped to grab a couple of things."

"Ok," I said. "I was hoping to spend a little time with you," I told her.

"We will be together all weekend," she told me as she was walking around the house and grabbing stuff. She walked out of the bathroom with the scalpel in her hand that I was holding when I woke up. "Hey, this was lying on the floor last night when I heard the glass break. I cut my toe on it when I came to check on you. Is it yours?"

I hesitated, "Yes. I use it to trim photos closer when I place them in the case file." I answered. I was lying to her. Before last night, I had never seen that scalpel. "It's the murder weapon," I said. I stopped talking quickly, I don't know why I said it. "I meant to say that I think that one like it may have been used as the murder weapon in our case."

"Did you say something, hun? I was on my phone."

"No, Andrea. I didn't say anything. Be careful. I'll see you tomorrow night after work," I told her as I kissed her. She walked out the door, and the lights of her car disappeared down my street. I was alone. I walked into my bathroom and looked into what was left of my mirror. A distorted image of me stared back. I turned away and turned the lights off.

"It's a good thing she didn't figure it out, Jack. You would have to kill her to keep her quiet. She never shuts up anyway."

"Go to Hell," I told the whisper from behind me.

"I'm already there, Jack. I just want you to join me there."

Chapter 3

Kill Him

I woke up the next morning with blood all over my sheets in my bed. "What the Hell?" I thought to myself as I looked at my hand for signs of bleeding. I wasn't bleeding. I started looking all around and found bloody clothes on the floor. I quickly picked the clothes up and placed them into a garbage bag and sealed it. I noticed bloody footprints across the floor in the house too. I grabbed some bleach and water, mixed it up, and cleaned the floor. After a hot shower, I walked out to my car and found the floor covered in blood as well. I made a phone call to a man I knew that detailed vehicles and explained that I had cut myself and had gotten blood on my floor of the car. He said he could clean it if I gave him an hour. I placed a trash bag on the floor and drove to his shop. As I was waiting for my car to be cleaned, my cell phone rang. It was my partner.

"We have another body. Same situation as before, it looks like she was killed by the same guy," Colby told me. "Are you coming in today?"

"No, Colb. I am still pretty sore in my hand. I am going to take the extra day. I'll be in tomorrow for sure."

"Ok, Partner. I'll see what the M.E. brings up. Oh, By the way, we have a witness. The sketch artist is with him now."

"A witness? What did he see?"

"He said he saw a younger blond guy. He said he saw the guy pull our victim into the alley, where we recovered the body. We'll be clearing the scene soon. Get better, Jack. Bye."

"Bye, Colb," I told her as my gut tightened up. I felt utterly sick to my stomach. I remembered having a dream last night. I had a dream that I was cutting up a woman.

"It wasn't a dream, Jack. You were cutting up that filthy wretch."

"I didn't kill anyone!" I shouted. "You did it, didn't you!"

"When you are sleeping, your body belongs to me. I can do whatever I want to. I wish you would sleep all of the time Jack; I have a lot of work to catch up on."

"You piece of garbage! You killed that girl!"

"You bet I did, Jack. I'll tell you another thing, you enjoyed it."

"Liar! I don't enjoy this! I am a cop for Christ's sake! What in the Hell are you?"

"I'm you, Jack. I am everything that you can't be when you are awake. I am what you secretly wish you could be, but you are too much of a sissy to let go. I am the darkness in your heart and your mind."

"I don't fantasize about death and killing women! I have sworn to protect people, not murder, and mutilate them!"

"Well, Jack, you are sure as Hell doing a fine job of it. You'll be the only cop in prison that has a medal of valor hanging in his cell. I am going to let you go now, Jack. You had better get to the police station. It sounds like we may have been seen last night. You might want to consider doing some damage control. See you tomorrow morning after we work all night again."

"I won't fall asleep, you bastard! I'll stay awake to keep you from hurting anyone else!"

"You'll try, and you'll fail. I have time, Jack. I have time."

"I won't sleep! Come back here and talk to me, you asshole!" He was gone. He had committed a murder and left me to take the entire blame. He was also right about one thing; I did have to consider damage control. I needed to get down to the station and find out what this witness saw.

I made it to the station about a half-hour after my car was finished. Colby was sitting at her desk, and I could hear the Captain yelling at someone on the phone in his office. I snuck over to Colby's desk and sat down, "What's the word, Colby? Do we have any leads?"

"The sketch artist just finished about 10 minutes ago. I was just going to talk with our witness," Colby told me.

"I'll do it, Colb. I want to see what he knows," I told her. I walked into the interview room, and I deliberately forgot to turn on the camera to record the conversation. The witness stared at me as though he had seen a ghost. "What did you see?" I asked him.

"I didn't see anything. It must be a mistake. I was drunk," he said as his voice trembled.

"That's what I thought you saw. If anyone asks, you had better get amnesia really quick. Get it?" I told him.

"I get it," he said. He was scared. "It was you. I saw you pull that girl into the alley. You came out covered in blood. You looked right at me and put your finger to your lips and told me SHHHH."

"Then why in the Hell aren't you doing it? If I catch you back here saying you witnessed anything, I'll be pulling you into an alley. It won't be nice and gentle like the girl either. They will need dental records to identify you. Understand?" I asked as I slammed him into the wall by his shirt. He walked out of the room, and Colby entered.

"Did he say anything?" she asked.

"It was a case of mistaken identity. He's a drunk, I don't think he knows what he saw."

"The Captain wants to see us," Colby informed me. We walked into the Captain's office, "You wanted to see us, sir?" I asked him.

"What in the hell are you doing in this picture by the sketch artist?" the Captain asked me.

"That witness is a drunk, sir. He thought it looked like me, but he said the guy had dark hair," I told him.

"Well, whatever it is, I want you both to give your other cases to Hernandez and Caffey. This case will take priority. I want this asshole caught. You both understand? We are taking heat from the top, the last victim was the Mayor's niece. It won't be very long before that information surfaces, so you better find him," he told us. "Hey Jack, that picture doesn't even look like you. The guy in it is better looking. Get your asses out of here."

"Yes, sir." We both answered as we exited his office. "I am heading home, Colby. I'm tired, and my hand is hurting. I'll catch you tomorrow."

"Ok, Jack. I agree with the Captain, by the way, that guy was better looking than you," Colby joked.

"Piss off, Colby. Good night," I said. I returned to my car and looked at the paperwork I had retrieved from the case. I heard a voice from behind me as I rifled through the paperwork looking for the address of the witness.

"You know he saw us. You know what you have to do."

"What do I have to do?" I asked as I looked into the rearview mirror. I observed red glowing eyes staring back into mine.

"Kill him." He told me.

Chapter 4

Animal Takes Form

As I sat outside of the address that the witness left, I started to doze off. I tried as hard as I could to stay awake in the car, but I couldn't. I began to dream. I dreamt about chasing the man that witnessed my new alter ego kill that girl. I dreamt that I chased him down and cornered him. I had my gun leveled at his face, and he was begging for his life. What was strange, I felt relaxed, like it was meant to be. I woke suddenly to realize that it wasn't a dream. I was, in fact, standing with my gun drawn with it level to the man's face. I noticed that his face was bleeding, and I could see he was scared. He was begging me not to shoot him.

"Kill him. Kill him now. You will be no good to me in a prison cell. Do it," I heard whispering from all around my head.

"No! I will not kill an innocent man," I said as I began to lower my gun. "This man cannot die for being in the wrong place at the wrong time."

"You still can't make the hard decisions, Jack," the whisper in my head said. "That's ok. I will," I heard it say as I felt my arm lift, and my finger began to tighten on the trigger.

"No!" I screamed as I fired off three rounds into the man's chest. I watched his body slump forward, and his eyes became glassy. I dropped my gun and ran to the man's side. I rolled him to his back. He was gasping for air as I knelt close to him. "It wasn't

295

me," I whispered to him as tears streamed down my face. He raised his hand and started to point over my right shoulder. I turned quickly to see a shadowy figure standing behind me. The only thing I could see was the red glowing eyes in the head of the shadow. I felt the man's hand fall onto my shoulder and then lifelessly fall to the ground. He coughed, and his eyes rolled back into his head. "I'm sorry," I said as I wept over him. I felt a hand on my shoulder, and I spun around. It was the shadow. Those eyes were close to mine, and I heard it whisper to me.

"Now you have to figure out what to do about this detective. You have to figure out how to keep us out of prison."

"You rotten son of a bitch. You killed an innocent unarmed man," I said.

"He wasn't that innocent, Jack. Look into his coat pocket," The shadow figure told me as I reached into the man's pocket and found a loaded .38 caliber snub revolver.

"After I threatened him at the police station, what did you expect?" I said.

"He had that gun before that, Jack. He has had that gun since he was going to use it to rob the girl that we killed. He was no better than us."

"No better than you," I whispered in despair. "He was no better than you."

"You did the world a favor, Jack. Quit being such a whiney bitch. You need to figure out what we need to do to get out of this. You're the detective, what should we do here?"

"I am going to call Colby, and I am going to let her come and arrest me. If I am in a cell, everybody will be safe from you," I told it.

"You get locked into a cell, and I'll make sure your ailing mother dies, and her soul gets taken by the being that is making all of this possible for me. You're a religious man Jack, a catholic. What do you think Hell looks like? I'll guarantee that your mother will know if you get caught. With that being said, detective, you had better think quickly."

I stood up, and looking into those red glowing eyes, "I know what Hell looks like, I'm in it right now." I saw the shadow move across the room and lay on top of the dead man. It sank into his body. The man immediately sat up and grabbed his gun that was lying on the floor beside him. I saw his eyes glow deep red as he pointed the gun at me. "What are you doing?"

"Giving you a reason to shoot me," He said as I heard the gun go off. I felt the bullet rip into my left shoulder as warm blood splashed on my neck and face. I heard the man's body hit the floor as the shadow was now standing over me. "The next time, you make your own alibi Jack," it said to me. "Pick up your cell phone and call 911 before you bleed out. We have too much work to do to lose you now."

I picked up my cell phone and called 911. "This is detective Jack Murphy. I have been shot." I told the dispatcher as I tried to stay conscious. "I killed the perp, I need help. I'm losing a lot of blood."

"I'm tracking your GPS detective. Stay with me. They're on their way." The dispatcher told me as she tried to keep me talking. "Detective? Detective, are you there?" I kept hearing her say.

"You'll live, Jack. I won't be far," I heard it say as it disappeared into the shadows of the night. I watched two reds eyes fade into the darkness as I began to lose consciousness. All I could hear was sirens as those eyes faded away, and everything went black.

The next thing I remember is seeing lights above me, and some doctor trying to explain to me what he was going to do to save my left arm. I drifted back out, and when I woke up, Andrea and Colby were standing in my room.

"Jack? Hi honey," Andrea said. "I'll go get the doctor," She said to Colby as I saw Colby nod.

"You scared us, partner," Colby said. "What would possess you to go and talk to that witness again by yourself?" She asked as she sat on my bed and held my hand.

"What would possess me?" I said as I looked and saw the shadow with two glowing red eyes standing in the corner of my hospital room behind Colby.

Chapter 5

I Don't Want You Dead

Three months had passed since the shooting. I was cleared by doctors to return to work. I returned, and it had also been three months since I had seen the shadow or heard the voice. The Captain had reassigned me to desk duty for the next couple of months, and Colby was still working our case until I returned to full duty. I asked her if there were any leads in the case, and she told me that since my accident, the murders had abruptly stopped. "I think it might just be the calm before the storm," she told me. I had a feeling she was right. I knew it was too good to be true. I knew that he would return, and it frightened me. I got home from work that night, and as fate would have it, my suspicions were correct. I walked into my house and placed my keys on the table when I heard him.

"How are you feeling, Jack?"

"I was feeling good until just now," I answered as I made my way to the mirror in my bathroom. "Where have you been?"

"Why, Jack? Did you miss me?" it answered.

"I was just wondering why the 3-month hiatus? Where were you?" I asked it as I glared intensely into the mirror. I saw the red glow in my eyes that seemed to replace the blue color that they usually were.

"I needed your body to heal Jack. I needed you to get better so I could continue my work," it taunted me.

"Your work is finished. You won't use me to kill anybody else," I warned it as I looked into the mirror.

"You will do what I want you to do, Jack. I control your body when you sleep. I let you enjoy your last three months of freedom. We will be killing girls every night from here on out. If you don't cooperate, I'll cut that pretty little girlfriend up into thousands of pieces and feed her to the fish in the river," it warned me back.

"You touch her, and I'll..."

"You'll do what, Jack?" it said as it cut me off. "You'll kill me? You will do as you are told. I don't care if you like it or not. Quit whining and accept it."

I pulled out my gun and placed it against my head, "I'll just kill myself, and it ends," I threatened.

"Jack!" It said as it began to laugh. "If I wanted you dead, I'd have just made you jump off one of the tall buildings in the city. I don't want you dead."

"What do you want?" I asked as I trembled holding the gun to my head.

"I want you to suffer. I want you to suffer for what your Father did to me," it said coldly.

"My father?" I asked as I dropped the gun. "What does this have to do with my father?"

"I can't get to him where he is. I took the next best thing, his only son," it told me, gleefully. "I told him I'd get my revenge. I told him as he sat there watching them kill me on that table. So I am here, Jack. Here to take my vengeance out on you."

"My father?" I asked again. "What are you talking about? Revenge? My father was a detective when I was a kid. He quit the department when I was 13."

"I remember when you were 13. I remember your dog. I remember your parents thinking you were psychotic. I was the one Jack. It was the first step in taking my revenge on the man that sent me to death row. We've had enough of traveling down memory lane Jack. Put the gun down and get some rest. We'll be killing soon."

"NO!" I said as I started to pull the trigger. "It ends now."

"Jack! Who are you talking to?" I heard Andrea say as the door to my house opened, and Andrea came in.

"OOPS! Busted!" it said as it laughed. "I'll be back soon. I guess you won't be pulling that trigger right now."

"Go to Hell," I said as I dropped the gun. I turned around as Andrea opened the bathroom door.

"Who were you talking to, Jack? I heard you all the way outside as I was walking up the driveway," Andrea asked me.

"I was on the phone with somebody Andrea," I told her. "What's going on? I thought you were coming over for dinner."

"I couldn't wait, Jack," she said with excitement in her voice.

"Couldn't wait for what?" I asked.

"I couldn't wait until we had dinner tonight to tell you," she answered. "I have great news, I'm pregnant!" she screamed as she hugged me. "We are going to have a baby!"

"That's great news," I said as my heart sank into my stomach. I looked into the mirror as Andrea hugged me. I watched as my eyes began to glow a deep red, and my reflection began to smile. "That's the best news I've heard all day."

Chapter 6

Revenge Reborn

"Jack Davidson, that guy was an animal. Your dad put him away, and he got the death penalty. Why are you asking about your old man's cases, kid?" the Captain asked me.

"No particular reason, sir. It is just that since dad died, I can't ask him about it. How old was I when this happened?" I asked.

"He busted Davidson around the time you were a kid. I think you were about 13 when they finally placed him on that table to meet his maker," the Captain replied.

"What was it that Davidson did, Cap?" I asked.

"He was cutting up prostitutes. He was a surgeon that went off his nut. He committed at least 14 murders before your old man finally got him," the Captain replied.

"Thanks, Cap," I said as I was exiting his office.

"Hey, kid. Your dad was never the same after that case. Don't let the case you and Colby are working on consume you."

"I'm trying Cap. Good night." I got into my car, and I heard his voice.

"Now you know who I am, does it make it easier for you, Jack?" it asked me.

"It just gives me the background. It makes me aware of the sick, twisted piece of garbage that I am dealing with," I told it.

"Do you think this gives you an edge Jack? Do you think you have leverage? My whole family is dead. I didn't care about them if they weren't. You have nothing you can do to get rid of me. I'll have my revenge," it told me.

"I don't care about what you want. I will stay awake and take whatever drug I need to make that happen. You may own me in my dreams, but you don't control me while I am awake," I told it.

"Jack, do you think that is how it works? Do you think I can physically control you? Do you think I did those horrible things to those whores? That was all you. I just planted the seed," it told me as it laughed.

"We'll see how comfortable you are in a few minutes," I told it. "We are taking a little drive somewhere. I've found somebody that can rid me of you." I laughed as I taunted it.

I began to drive. It tried to get me to continue the useless banter the entire time I was driving. I just ignored it. I pulled up to the church I grew up in, I hadn't been back since my dad's funeral.

"Jack, if you go into that church and do what I think you are going to do, I will promise you… you'll regret it for the rest of your life. I will make sure of that," it warned me.

"You'll be going back to Hell in a few minutes. Father Kirkpatrick is trained in getting rid of evil spirits. He'll be sending you back to where you belong," I warned it back. I walked into the church, and I felt better instantly. I heard him plead with me as I kept walking toward the alter, and I dropped to my knees and prayed. Father Kirkpatrick met me there, and we began.

"Jack, you'll regret this. You haven't seen Hell yet. I promise that you will never live a peaceful life after this, I'll take everything. This is your last warning. Stop this," it pleaded with me.

"Go to Hell, Jack," I said smugly. Father Kirkpatrick performed his exorcism of it and told me that I should have no further issues. If I did, he told me to come back. I thanked him and shook his hand.

I saw Father later that year when Andrea and I were married by him and later when our daughter was born. I felt like I had a new lease on life. I no longer took anything for granted. Two years had passed, and Jack Davidson was just a horrible memory. Every once in a while, I would think about the women that died at my hand because of Davidson. I would pray for them and the man I killed because of that monster. I prayed that I would be forgiven for my sins and that we would be able to raise our daughter and our family for the rest of our lives. One night I came home and had just finished showering when I found a message on my phone to call Colby. I picked up the phone and called her, "Hey, Colby. What's going on?" I asked her.

"Jack? Where are you?" She asked me.

"I am home, Colby. I just got here. What is going on?" I asked her.

"I'm sorry, Jack," she said as her voice trembled. "Andrea is here with me. She has your backup weapon. She asked me to call you."

"Colby? What is going on? Are you both ok?" I asked, concerned. I heard the gunshot over the phone. "Colby? Colby!" I started to scream. "My God, Colby! Answer me!"

"She's dead, Jack," I heard Andrea's voice on the other end of the phone. "So is Father Kirkpatrick. I sure they will find him soon. I cut him up just like we cut up those whores a few years ago."

"Andrea? What are you saying?" I asked.

Then I heard his voice. "I warned you that you would regret going into that church, Jack. Now I've taken your priest, your partner, and your wife," it said. "I just wonder if you can make it to the daycare before I get there. Let me see Jack. You are 25 minutes from there, and I am 15 minutes from there. I hope you get there in time."

"Don't you touch my daughter, you deranged asshole. I'll send you to Hell," I promised.

"No, Jack, I've just sent you there. Hope to see you at the daycare. I've missed you," it said as I heard the phone go dead.

DAN NORVELL

Chapter 7

He Got His Revenge

I raced through traffic as I was on the phone with the dispatcher. "Send them now!" I screamed. "My wife has just killed my partner. She is going for my daughter!" I told them as I gave them the address and drove wildly through traffic.

"We are sending them now, Jack. Slow down. You can't help your daughter if you are dead," the dispatcher tried to tell me. I hung the phone up, and it started to ring again. I looked down, and it was Andrea's number.

I heard my wife on the phone, "Jack. Jack, I'm sorry. I don't know what is happening. Jack, I shot Colby. I killed Father Kirkpatrick. What the Hell is wrong with me?" she asked me, crying.

"Andrea, it isn't you. I am so sorry," I told her. "Andrea, I love you."

"I love you too," I heard her say as her voice changed from her sweet voice to a sick and deranged voice that belonged to Davidson.

"Hi, honey. We are already here playing with Chelsea. She's beautiful. She looks like your Mom," it told me.

"Don't hurt my daughter," I pleaded. "Don't hurt my little girl."

"I've already hurt your little girl, both of them," it said. "I'll see you in a few minutes, Jack," it said as I heard the phone go dead.

My phone was ringing, and I could see it was the Captain calling. I ignored it as I arrived at the daycare. I could hear sirens in the distance as I drew my gun and ran into the building.

"Where are you?" I screamed as I ran through the corridor, going to the room where my daughter was always dropped off. I entered the room, and my wife was holding our daughter in her arms, along with my gun in her hand. The daycare worker was lying dead with a gunshot wound to her head. "Andrea? Put Chelsea down, honey. You control your actions, not him."

"Jack. I'm sorry. I love you both," she said, crying. All at once, her voice became deeper, and I heard Davidson begin to speak as her eyes began to glow a deep red.

"Well, Jack, here we are," he said. "You know, they say that revenge is sweet. How much sweeter can it be than when it is taken on the child of the one I hate."

"Let them go. Take me instead," I pleaded.

"That priest marked you, Jack. I can't come back to you. This is suiting me much better anyway," it said as it aimed the gun at my daughter's face. "You have a choice to make Jack. Lose them both, or just one of them. I am going to count to three. When I get to three, I am going to fire this weapon at your daughter. You either have to shoot me, or I am going to kill her."

"Don't do this, Davidson. I am begging you."

"Get bent, Jack. After I kill your daughter, they will convict your wife and give her the same lethal injection they gave me. You lose both ways. So, you have to ask yourself, Jack, does she die now by your bullet, or do they both die? You make the call. 1."

"Davidson, don't do this," I pleaded.

"2," he said as he cocked the hammer on the gun.

"I'm sorry, Andrea," I said.

"Thhhr," He started to say as I heard the gunshot.

I pulled the trigger as I watched my wife's body hit the floor, and I ran to grab my daughter. She was fine. She didn't have a scratch on her. I turned to look at my wife lying lifeless on the floor. I heard the other officers entering the room as the tears streamed down my face, and I kissed my daughter on the head over and over. "I'm sorry, I'm so sorry," I said over and over.

"Jack," I heard the Captain say as he placed his hand on my shoulder. "It's over kid."

"It is over," I wept. "He got his revenge."

"Who, Jack?" The Captain asked.

"Davidson," I whispered through my tears. I handed my daughter to the Captain as I hit the ground and began to wail. I held my wife's hand until they came and took her body away.

I woke up at night, hearing his voice in my room. I would stare at the empty pillow in my bed next to me and think about what he took from my daughter and me. He had stained us both with the blood of every victim he took. The stain that was the worst was the stain of my own wife's blood on my hands. I cleaned out Colby's locker about two months after everything happened. I found some reports she had not filed when the murders had taken place years back. She suspected me but couldn't prove it.

DAN NORVELL

Chapter 8

Killing Again

One night, about 3 in the morning, my cell phone went off. The Captain told me that a girl had been murdered and left in an alleyway. He asked if I would be willing to take the case. I told him I'd have to get my mother to come and sit with my daughter, and I would be there as soon as I could be. I finally made it to the crime scene, and on one of the building walls written in blood from the victim were the words, "Detective Murphy, it will never be over." I walked away and called the Captain. "He's back," I told him. "He's back, and he's taunting me, Captain."

"Calm down, Jack," the Captain told me. "I'll have someone drive you home, and we'll talk about it tomorrow."

"Ok, Captain," I answered back reluctantly. "I'll talk to you then."

"Get some sleep, kid. Goodnight," he said.

"I will," I said. I knew by the tone in his voice that he thought I had returned too early. He thought I was going off of my nut. I locked my car, and one of the officers told me the Captain wanted him to drive me home. We drove through the city and towards my house.

I was half asleep when I noticed that we had turned around and were now headed back toward the city. "Officer? What are we doing?" I asked, confused.

"I have something to show you. I wouldn't move if I were you detective." He said as I noticed his gun was drawn and pointed at me.

"What is going on?" I asked again. All at once, I heard his voice as the eyes of the officer driving the car began to glow red.

"Hello, Jack," I heard him say as he pushed harder on the gas. I listened to the engine roar as we picked up speed. "It's been a while."

"Screw you, Davidson," I said. "Are you going to kill me finally?"

"No, Jack," he said as he began laughing. "I'm driving back into the city, and we are going to have some fun together. I am going to show you how much fun it is to kill those whores."

"No, Davidson," I told him. "Kill me now. I won't have any part in your sick twisted games anymore."

"You'll do as you're told, Jack. If you don't, I'll go and kill your mother and daughter tonight," he said. He pulled out the handcuffs on his belt and told me to place them onto my wrists. "Put them on, Jack. I don't want you interfering with our fun. If you don't, I'll shoot you in the stomach, drive to your house and drag your mother out by the hair and cut her to pieces starting at her feet while you watch," he warned me.

"You are a sick bastard," I told him as I placed the handcuffs onto my wrists.

"You might be right, Jack. I am a sick bastard. I am also the bastard that decides what kind of life I am going to allow the son of my jailer to have left," he told me.

"My father was doing his job!" I said. "It was his job to keep psychos like you off of the street."

"It was my job to clean up the streets from that disgusting filth that is on every corner, Jack!" he scolded me. "Your father took that from me. He took everything. Since he's dead now, I can only take my revenge on his family. It's only fitting that you are also a stinking cop. It makes it twice as sweet for me."

He kept talking and telling me what he planned to do to the rest of the women that he would be killing in the near future. We arrived back in the city, and he parked the car at the end of a dark alley. He placed me into the back of the car, so I could not escape.

"You stay here, Jack. I'm going to show you how it feels to watch one of them die. It's exciting."

"Let me go, you sick son of a bitch!" I said. "I don't want any part of your deranged game."

"You are a part of it, Jack," he told me. "I don't care if you like it or not. Now sit there and shut your mouth or I'll shut it for you," he said as he disappeared into the shadows of the alleyway. Within a few minutes, I heard a woman screaming, and I watched in absolute horror as he dragged her all the way down to the car by her hair.

"Here she is, Jack!" he said gleefully. I began to pound on the window and yell to him to stop as I heard the woman scream. I felt sick to my stomach as I listened to her screams become gurgling and then silence. He walked over to the car and opened the back door and threw something in at me. I felt the blood splash across my face as I looked down onto the floor to see the woman's head lying on it. I began to vomit as he got back into the driver's seat, and we began to move again. "Someday soon, Jack, I'll be sending you the body parts of your mother," he taunted.

"I'll stop you. So help me God, I will send you back to Hell," I promised.

"Stop being such a sissy and accept it, Jack. You should feel honored. I have given you a glimpse into the mind of a genius," he told me.

"All I have seen is a sick and twisted sack of garbage. You're crazy, and you deserved to die," I said.

"Screw you, Jack!" He said as he floored the car. "You'll have a tough time explaining this one." He drove faster and faster toward the waterfront; he wasn't slowing down. "I hope you can swim with handcuffs on Jack."

He drove the car off the waterfront dock, and I heard the car hit the water. I leaned back into the seat and began to kick the window of the car door as hard as I could. I felt water rush in as I struggled to get through the window I had just kicked out. I swam as hard as I could to make it to the dock. I finally made it and grabbed for one of the ladder rungs going out of the water as I turned to watch the car sink into the darkness and depths of the water. I felt somebody swim up beside me, and I looked to see the officer that Davidson had taken over swim up to me. He looked confused and bewildered.

"Are you ok?" I asked him.

"Yes, detective. What are we doing here?" he asked.

"It's a long story. Help me out of the water and take these cuffs off of me," I told him. He did so, and as he was reaching for his handcuff key, I saw his eyes begin to glow red again. He smiled as he reached for my gun on my side and pulled it out and pressed it to the side of his head.

"As I said, Jack, you'll have a heck of a time explaining this one," he said as he fired the gun.

"No!" I screamed as I watched the young officers' body slump to the dock. I heard sirens coming closer as I struggled to do CPR on him. I saw the dock light up as squad cars pulled up and shined their lights down on us. I stopped doing CPR as one of the officers came up to me and placed his hand on my shoulder.

"Detective, you are under arrest," he said as he pulled me to my feet. I was placed into the back of a squad car as the rest of the officers were securing the scene. I stared into the first light of the new morning as I watched a shadow with red glowing eyes disappear into the cracks of the dock. Davidson had finally gotten his revenge.

About The Authors

Dan Norvell grew up in a small farming community in Northern Illinois. Dan worked at his family's cattle farm until it closed in 1990. Dan also spent several years in the Fire Service earning many different certifications and taking on leadership roles within the service. During that time Dan also spent some of those years as a Paramedic. It was his time in the Fire Service on the Ambulance where Dan experienced many miracles and tragedies. Dan ended his days in the Fire Service in 2009. It was later in 2009 when Dan decided to take his hobby that began in 1996 of investigating the paranormal to the mainstream and started his paranormal team. In 2010 he met his partner Larry Eissler and there has been no stopping them since. It is through those experiences that Dan has loosely based some of his fictional writings. Dan currently resides back in his hometown where he is married with two children.

Larry Eissler grew up in the northwest suburbs of Chicago, Illinois and currently resides in his hometown with his son Aiden. At the age of 18, Larry enlisted in the Army National Guard as a 74D Chemical Operations Specialist and served on the Northern Illinois CERFP until his deployment to Afghanistan in 2008. Returning from his deployment in the Fall of 2009, Larry began an interest in the

paranormal that would eventually introduce him to Dan Norvell in the Spring of 2010. Since then, Larry and Dan have investigated together for over ten years, visited hundreds of haunted locations, and documented their findings for their followers.

Other Haunted Road Media titles from Dan Norvell and Larry Eissler:

Paranormal investigators Dan Norvell and Larry Eissler take you inside a unique perspective of the Black Hawk War, a conflict between the United States and the Native American Sauk war chief, Black Hawk. While conveying the oft-overlooked history of these battles, they also explore the reported hauntings at the war's historic landmarks. Discover a time in Illinois's history rife with despair and tragedy that has produced a significant amount of paranormal activity.

Haunted Road Media
www.hauntedroadmedia.com

www.ingramcontent.com/pod-product-compliance
Lightning Source LLC
Chambersburg PA
CBHW020840060726
PP18531500001B/6